BOOKS BY ERIC WALTERS

Full Court Press
Rebound
Caged Eagles
The Bully Boys
The Money Pit Mystery
Three-on-Three
Visions
Tiger by the Tail
The Hydrofoil Mystery
War of the Eagles
Stranded
Diamonds in the Rough
Trapped In Ice
STARS
Stand Your Ground

THE MONEY PIT MYSTERY

ERIC WALTERS

THE MONEY PIT MYSTERY

HarperCollins*PublishersLtd*

www.harpercanada.com

HarperCollins books may be purchased for
educational, business, or sales promotional
use. For information please write:
Special Markets Department,
HarperCollins Canada,
55 Avenue Road, Suite 2900,
Toronto, Ontario, Canada M5R 3L2

First HarperCollins massmarket ed.
ISBN 0-00-648156-6

Canadian Cataloguing in Publication Data

Walters, Eric, 1957–
The money pit mystery

ISBN 0-00-648156-6

I. Oak Island Treasure Site (N.S.) –
    Juvenile fiction.
I. Title

PS8595.A598M65 2001   jC813'.54
C00-932471-2
PZ7.W17129Mo 2001

01 02 03 04 OPM 6 5 4 3 2 1

Printed and bound in the United States

For Anita, Christina,
Nick and Julia . . .
the true treasures
in my life

THE MONEY PIT
MYSTERY

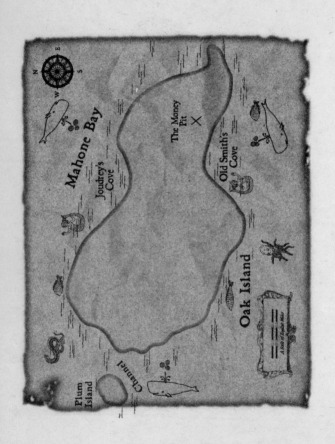

Chapter One

I shuffled the deck of cards and then cut. Next I dealt five cards onto the bench beside me. I flipped over the top card; it was the ace of hearts. I smiled to myself. It was where I'd put it in the deck, sixth from the top. For the trick to work it had to be in exactly the right place. Carefully, I gathered up the cards and repositioned the ace in the correct spot.

"Beth, can I show you a trick?" I asked my sister.

"Leave me alone, Sam," she answered without taking her head out of her hands.

"But it's a good trick. You'll want to see it!"

"All I want to see is the end of this boat ride," she muttered.

"You're not enjoying the ride?"

She burped and moaned slightly.

I guess she wasn't. The ferry ride was only an hour

long, but as soon as we'd left the harbour and headed for the open seas it had gotten really rough. We'd been bounced around pretty good. I just thought it was sort of like an extra-long roller coaster, and I love riding roller coasters.

My sister didn't like amusement park rides. She said she'd be quite happy to ride a roller coaster if they let her drive. That wasn't likely. She even insisted on riding in the front seat of the car because she said she got "motion sick." I always figured she was just saying that so she could sit up front and fiddle with the radio or because that was as close as she could get to being behind the wheel herself. My sister definitely liked to be in charge.

I didn't remember the ferry ever affecting her this way before, but I also didn't remember the ride ever being this rough on any of our other trips. Of course, maybe I wasn't remembering right because it had been almost three years since our last time aboard. Looking at Beth now, her face a strange shade of grey, I was beginning to believe that maybe she hadn't been kidding all along about a weak stomach.

I shuffled the deck again. "Come on, it's a good trick. It'll take your mind off things."

"It isn't my mind I want off of things. It's my stomach."

"Just try. Cut the deck and—"

"If you don't leave me alone Sam *I'll* show you a trick."

"A trick? What sort of a trick?"

"I'll make something appear . . . all over your

shoes," she said as she belched loudly and covered her mouth. "Or better still, I'll make an eleven-year-old brat disappear . . . over the side of the boat."

"Beth, be nice to your little brother," Mom warned as she walked up unexpectedly. She'd been outside on the deck.

"I'm trying to be nice."

"Then try harder. You both promised not to fight and bicker. You said you'd get along the way you used to get along."

"*I'm* getting along," I said smugly, smirking at Beth.

"We never got along," Beth answered.

She lifted her head off her hands long enough to give me a nasty look. Without her saying a word I knew what she was thinking—"you little suck up." She always accused me of trying to get on Mom's good side, doing things to please her, being a "mama's boy." Maybe that was true, but only compared to Beth. Lately she seemed to go out of her way to fight with Mom. It should have been the two of them who promised to try to get along.

They were always bickering about something. I just kept my head down and tried to stay out of the way when they got into one of their real fights. And there'd been a lot of them lately.

Beth was only thirteen, but lately she'd been acting like she thought she was a lot older. She'd started wearing make-up and was caught skipping school. Mom nearly killed her for that—nothing bothers a teacher more than having one of her own kids cut classes.

The worst fights, though, were about Brent. Brent was Beth's "boyfriend." Mom said Beth could have "boys who were friends," but she was much too young to have a "boyfriend." And even if she did have a boyfriend it shouldn't be somebody who was three years older than she was. After fighting about it for two whole days, and then not talking at all for another two, they reached an agreement: Beth would pretend she didn't have a boyfriend, and Mom would pretend not to notice that she did. Maybe it wasn't the most honest arrangement, but I didn't care because it stopped them from fighting, at least for a day or two.

I leaned close to Beth. "Too bad Brent isn't here to see you," I whispered, so softly that Mom couldn't hear me.

She looked up at me but didn't say a word.

"He would never have seen you looking so lovely."

She opened her mouth to say something and then closed it again. Silence from Beth . . . now that was something I didn't hear very often. She must really be sick. I felt bad.

"Remember when we were little," I said, "and we used to think the ride was really long because we couldn't wait to get to the island?"

Beth didn't answer.

"And we used to talk about all the things we wanted to do when we got there. Do you remember?"

She chuckled a bit, and then slowly and slightly nodded her head.

"And we'd go to the beach and spend almost all our time there swimming and making sand castles and running through the dunes and playing games and pretending and imagining all sorts of things. Do you remember?"

"Of course I do," she said softly.

"And on the way back we'd stop at the Dairy Queen for a cone, or the bakery for fresh-out-of-the-oven buns or fresh-made doughnuts," I continued.

"Please," Beth said, holding up a hand. "No talk about food . . . please."

"Sorry."

"How much longer?" she asked.

"I could see the harbour when I was up top. We can't be more than ten minutes out now," Mom answered. "Maybe you'd feel better if you came topside. Sometimes the spray hitting your face helps."

"Nothing can help," Beth said forlornly.

"Come, it can't hurt," Mom suggested. She took one of Beth's arms and helped her to her feet. Beth didn't protest and Mom held on to her arm as they stumbled across the shifting floor. I watched until they disappeared through the hatch leading to the deck.

I cast my eyes around the interior of the boat. Almost all the seats were empty. Most of the passengers were up on deck looking at the sights. Of the few people inside, a couple were talking, one man was asleep under his hat and a woman appeared to be suffering the same fate as my sister.

I couldn't help thinking back to all the times I'd been on this ferry before. I thought of one of the first trips I could recall and remembered how big the ferry seemed and how scary it was to travel out on the ocean and how excited I felt to be going out to see Grandpa. From way before I could remember until I was eight we used to go out to the island every summer to spend a week or two with him. Once we stayed almost the whole summer.

That was the summer I learned to ride my bike— Grandpa showed me. It wasn't easy keeping the wheels straight on the sand-covered dirt roads, but at least when I fell it didn't hurt much. Grandpa ran after me each time, holding on to the back of my seat—back and forth up and down that street until he was wheezing like an engine. But he wouldn't give up, and he wouldn't let me give up until I could ride.

And that wasn't all that we did together. He used to take me fishing, almost every day, and play catch with me and at night he'd tell me stories. Not from a book, but from his head. Stories filled with adventure and pirates, the mysterious Money Pit of Oak Island, and how someday he and I would find the buried treasure of Captain Kidd.

I couldn't think of Oak Island without thinking of buried treasure. Ever since I was old enough to remember, the bedtime stories Grandpa told me each night were about treasure. They were so much different than the stories Mom told and they were ingrained in my head . . . it was almost like something I'd seen instead of just something I'd been told. I loved his stories. And my favourite was about the treasure of Captain Kidd . . . buried deep in the Money Pit. The Money Pit was the most famous place on Oak Island.

It was a deep, deep hole, so deep that no one had ever reached the bottom . . . the place where the treasure was buried.

I took a deep breath and my whole body shuddered with a deep sigh. I hadn't seen him for three years. Boy I missed him.

During our last visit to Oak Island, three summers ago, Beth and I were woken up by the sounds of Mom and Grandpa arguing in the other room. In the morning, Mom ordered us to pack and we took the ferry home, even though we weren't supposed to leave for another week. We asked Mom why, but she wasn't in a mood to explain. We hardly even had a chance to say goodbye to Grandpa because we rushed out so fast. And then we didn't come back again. Not that summer, or the next or the next. Sure, we sent him some letters and he sent a few back to us. And a couple of times a year, at Christmas and on our birthdays, he called us on the phone.

I tried to talk to Mom about what had happened and how much I missed him, but it really didn't do much good. The little she did say was how "difficult" Grandpa could be, and how "opinionated and stubborn" he was, and how I wouldn't understand how hard it was to be raised by somebody like him. I lived with her so I guess I had a pretty good idea. She was the person in the whole world who most reminded me of him. Of course, I'd never tell her that. Just like I couldn't ever talk to her about how much I missed Dad . . . or missed the bits I could remember about him . . . he'd been gone since I was really small. At least having Grandpa around in the summers made up for it a little. Until he was gone as well.

I guess that's what made this trip so strange. It was like we weren't even supposed to mention Grandpa for three whole years and then we get a phone call and, bang, we pack up everything and leave immediately for Oak Island. Mom didn't explain a lot except to say we had to go and Grandpa wasn't "doing" so well. Beth thought the whole thing was just an excuse to separate her from Brent and . . . what was the point in thinking about any of this stuff? It wasn't like I could change it or even understand it.

I shuffled the cards noisily, cut them again and started dealing to three imaginary players. Each time I dealt a card to myself I pulled it off the bottom of the pack. I was getting so good it was almost impossible to tell what I was doing. A big part of a lot of card tricks is being able to draw from the bottom of the deck.

The boat's horn sounded out loudly to signal we were coming into the town dock. I quickly gathered up the cards and stuffed them in my pocket. I reached down, grabbed my bag and slung it on my shoulder. It didn't just carry my clothes but also contained some of my favourite magic tricks. It would be neat to show Grandpa all my tricks. It was always good to have a new audience to perform for. And besides, he was the one who showed me my very first magic trick.

Mom had left her and Beth's bags here. I wanted to go up on deck but couldn't leave their luggage behind. I lifted up Mom's case and slung it over my other shoulder. I was annoyed when Mom said we had to "pack light" and wouldn't let us take much stuff, but now as I was lifting the bags I was grateful. With my free hand I grabbed Beth's suitcase. It was the biggest and, I realized as I tried to lift it, the heaviest. Mom had said that she'd allowed Beth to take more stuff because clothes were more important to a thirteen-year-old girl. I didn't mind . . . well, I didn't mind until I tried to lift it . . . after all, the only things I was planning on needing were my bathing suit, towel and, of course, my magic tricks and magic books.

I half-lifted, half-dragged the bags across the floor. I could tell we'd already entered the town's harbour because the boat was hardly bouncing at all. Thank goodness. I didn't think I could manage all three bags and a bucking boat too.

"You want a hand with those?" one of the crew members asked.

"No, I can handle it," I answered instantly.

He nodded and was off up the stairs leading to the deck before I had a chance to reconsider his offer. Why didn't I let him help? Why did I always say no whenever anybody offered to help me? That didn't matter now though. All that mattered was getting these bags up to the deck. I muscled them across the floor and half-carried, half-bumped them up the steps. As soon as I hit the deck, I saw Beth and Mom. They were standing against the rail just off to the side of the hatch. I dumped the bags at their feet and took a spot beside Mom on the railing. I looked over at them. Beth's face had better colour and didn't seem so pained. Both she and Mom were staring ahead at the approaching town that stretched out in front of us, curving all around the harbour. Dead ahead was the pier.

I couldn't help but think about all the times Grandpa had been there waiting for us when our boat arrived. He always had a little present or two for me and Beth. Nothing fancy, but always something interesting. And he'd tell me how much I'd grown and say to Beth how she was getting prettier every year— okay, so he didn't always tell the truth about everything.

I knew I just wanted to run up and give him a big hug. Of course, that would just give Beth something else to make fun of me about. And what about Mom? Would she be upset because they were still mad at each other . . . no, they had to have made up or we wouldn't be coming here.

Mom sighed deeply.

"Are you okay?" I asked.

"Yes, I'm fine. It just brings back so many memories. Even though I haven't been here for a few years it'll always be my home. It all looks so familiar. I guess not that much changes here."

Maybe not much, but the only thing I was really looking for wasn't there. I'd scanned up and down the whole pier. This time, I couldn't see Grandpa waiting for us.

Chapter Two

The ferry bumped into the dock and the crew members tied it into place against the gigantic rubber tractor tires that protected and cushioned the boat as it bounced against the pier. I scanned up and down again. He had to be here. He was always here to meet us. Maybe I just couldn't see him among the other people who were on the pier, either waiting to get on, or there to meet somebody else.

The big back doors were lowered, forming a bridge for the cars to drive off and for other passengers like us, without cars, to walk off the vessel. A thick knot of passengers formed and inched its way toward the exit while the cars and trucks and RVs rolled off.

Mom didn't like crowds and so there was no point in me even picking up my bag. We wouldn't be going anywhere until there was a clear path off the boat. I knew that even if she let us go and we left right away and squeezed through the crowd we wouldn't gain any more than a couple of minutes. Still, it would have been neat to try to be the first off and beat all the other people. I contented myself by continuing to search the dwindling crowd for Grandpa. The last car exited and the crowd was reduced to the last few stragglers.

"Let's get going," Mom said.

Beth picked up her bag and grunted. "Can somebody help me with my bag?" she asked weakly.

"There are only two other 'somebodies' here and we both have bags of our own," I answered sharply. "Maybe you shouldn't have packed so much junk."

"The only junk that was packed is all those stupid magic tricks in your bag and—"

"Please, both of you stop right now! I can't handle you two fighting. Here, Beth, you take my bag and I'll take yours," Mom offered.

"But that's not . . ." I started to protest.

"Yes, it is fair," Mom cut in. "Beth was sick so I've offered to help her. Do you have a problem with that?"

I did, but I wasn't stupid enough to argue anymore. "Do you have a problem with that?" is Mom talk for shut up and stop fighting or else.

"Good, now let's get going."

We picked up our bags and moved to the walkway. It was official, we were clearly the last passengers to leave the boat. We were so late our feet had hardly hit the pier when a crew member swung the gate to the side to allow people and vehicles to board the ferry for the return trip back to the mainland.

"I still don't see Grandpa," I said.

"I wouldn't imagine that you would," Mom said.

"But why not? He's always here to meet us," I said.

"He doesn't know we're coming."

"He doesn't?" A wave of disappointment and confusion flooded over me. "But why not?" I questioned.

"I don't want to go into that right now," she answered.

"But if he's not here then how do we get to his place?" Beth asked.

"Walk," Mom answered.

"Walk! If you knew Grandpa wasn't going to be here then why didn't we take our car across on the ferry?" Beth asked.

"Because it costs money, a lot of money, to bring across a car, especially a car we won't be needing while we're on the island."

"But it's a long way to Grandpa's place," she argued.

"Don't be silly. It's only a few blocks. When I was your age I walked this route every day."

"Carrying a suitcase?"

"Carrying groceries and other things that weighed even more than your bag," Mom countered.

There was hardly ever a point in arguing with Mom, and no point at all when it involved money. We weren't poor—or at least I didn't think we were poor, Mom was a grade five teacher—but there never seemed to be much money. And I didn't think anything bothered Mom as much as being reminded that we didn't have much cash.

We started up the gentle slope of the main street. Stores, brightly painted in greens and reds and yellows, lined both sides of the road. Most of them weren't what Grandpa called "real" stores. For him a real store was one that sold groceries, or hardware, or maybe clothes, or other things people needed. Instead, almost all the stores along the street had cute names like "The Treasure Chest" and "The Sea Dog" and only sold souvenirs and crafts and artsy things for the tourists who crowded along the narrow sidewalk. There seemed to be more of those fancy stores these days and fewer of the real kind. The sidewalks seemed more crowded with people bumping along on the narrow sidewalk. It was hard to get through with our bags. I guess there were a few people along the street who actually lived here on the island, but most of the people we passed came equipped with cameras and little guide books. Tourists. Grandpa hated tourists. The first time I heard him say that I was only little, and I thought he meant us too because we only came over for a few weeks every summer. Grandpa settled that quick. He said that not only were we not tourists but that we weren't even visitors. We belonged on the island, and we were really just visitors on the mainland, and someday we'd come back for good. That would have been something, to live on the island.

It wasn't that I minded where we lived. It was pretty good . . . with the exception of a few jerks at my school. But Beth said there were jerks everywhere. It was just that the island was special. Maybe we never lived there but it always felt like home to me.

A different smell than the ocean breeze caught my attention. Directly across the street was Murray's Bakery. Thank goodness Murray's hadn't become another souvenir stand. I turned to say something to Mom and Beth, but I noticed that both of them had also been captured by the escaping aroma and were gazing in that direction.

Mom looked at me and smiled. "I think that would be a good idea," she said in answer to my unasked question. "Beth, are you up for something to eat?"

"Murray's isn't just 'something,'" she said with a smile. "My stomach can definitely handle something from there."

"Excellent. Let's go. Sam, give me your hand," Mom said as we started to cross the street.

"Come on, Mom, I'm almost twelve years old!" I protested.

"And I'm over forty so listen to what I say," she replied as she slung the suitcase over to her other side and grabbed my hand.

The streets were crowded with cars, but they were all moving pretty slowly and we easily shuffled through them to reach the other side.

"This place has good memories," Mom said.

"And good doughnuts," Beth added.

"Both," Mom agreed. "And believe me, over the years I've had more of both than the two of you combined."

Mom pushed through the screen door, tripping a bell attached above the door. I inhaled deeply. The smell outside, the little trickles that had escaped through the screen, were nothing compared to those inside.

The store was almost as crowded as the sidewalk and I side-stepped people to move closer to the nearest display case. It was only half-filled, the rest gone from the morning rush when everything would have been still steaming hot, fresh out of the ovens. But still, half of heaven was pretty good.

Mom took a number and we looked longingly at the remaining treats while we waited for the numbers ahead of us to be taken care of. I watched each of those people being served and imagined how good their selection would be. I changed my mind about what I wanted three times while I was staring at the things being put in other people's bags. Finally I decided. I couldn't possibly do better than a sticky bun and a gingerbread man—the things I'd had almost every day the last summer we were here.

"Number sixty-eight!" called out the woman behind the counter.

Mom stepped forward and held out the little wedge of paper.

"So what can we get for you . . ." the woman asked, stopping in mid-sentence. "My Lord, it's little Becky Simmons!"

"Hi, Mrs. O'Connor."

"It's so good to see you!" She rushed out around the counter and gave my mother a big hug. "It's been a long time since you've been on the island."

"About three years," Mom answered softly. She looked nervous and unsure of herself.

"Three years . . . well that's three years longer than it should be between visits. And these two strapping big children have grown so much since I last saw them."

"They have grown. These are Beth—"

"And Samuel," Mrs. O'Connor cut in. "No need to remind me of what I haven't forgot. I remember them both well from all the summers they spent here on the island. And of course the way your father's always in here carrying on about his grandchildren would make it hard to forget them." She paused and a worried look overtook her. "It's sad we don't see much of your father these days."

Mom bit on her lower lip. That was a sure sign she was worried.

Mrs. O'Connor craned her neck to one side to look behind us to the growing crowd of customers waiting to be served.

"Wait a second will you," she said. She turned around, took two steps and poked her head through the curtain that separated the store from the back room.

"Gwen! Come on out here for a moment and help serve the customers!" she called out.

Within a few seconds a young girl, not much older

than Beth, pushed through the curtain. She was wearing an apron and her hands, face and hair were covered with a film of flour. Mrs. O'Connor moved over to one side and crooked her finger for us to follow.

"I'm glad you're here for a few reasons," she said quietly. "Not just that it's nice to see you and your children, but I've been worried . . . worried about your father. I hope you don't think me too forward, or that I'm poking my nose where it doesn't belong, but . . ."

"It's all right, Mrs. O'Connor." Mom turned to Beth and me. "Could you excuse us for a minute, please."

"Excuse you, what did you . . ." I stopped myself. Of course I knew what she meant; she wanted to talk to Mrs. O'Connor alone.

Beth and I took a few steps in one direction while the two of them side-stepped the other way. I may have been looking at the treats behind the glass counter but my ears were aimed directly at where they stood and started talking. Why was everything a big secret anyway? Was she going to say something about Grandpa? Was he okay? I couldn't bear to even think that he wasn't.

"Dr. Robinson called to tell me about the situation," Mom said in such a hushed voice that I could only barely make out her words over the other sounds in the store.

So that was who the phone call was from. I'd just assumed it was Grandpa, up until him not being there at the dock.

"I was hoping he might," Mrs. O'Connor said. "You know how it is in a place like this. Busy as heck for three months of the year when all the tourists are flocking all around, but the rest of the year there's only us islanders and we pretty well know everything about everybody else. It's not just me who's worried about your father."

"What's he really like?" Mom asked anxiously.

"It's not like he's any one thing, really. Sometimes he seems to hardly remember things, even big things, like my name. Other times I don't see him, nobody does, must be just staying inside that little house of his. Then one day he'll be in here and it'll be like old times and he's joking and talking and laughing and I'd swear he was just like his old self again! Of course, that's part of the problem . . . your father's always been a little . . . a little . . ."

"I know," Mom interrupted. "He's always been more than a little different."

"I don't mean no offence. We all care dearly for your father. I just think that's maybe why it took so long for people to notice. Behaviour that would be strange in anybody else might just be your father being himself." She paused. "Maybe I should take your order so you can get on up to the house to see him."

"I'd like some sticky buns," I piped in eagerly before I realized I wasn't supposed to be listening to what they were saying.

Mom cast me a hard look for a few seconds and I looked down at the floor.

"I guess we'll start with a half dozen . . . no, make that a full dozen sticky buns," Mom began. "And a loaf of bread . . . do you have any egg bread left?"

"None in the display cases but I have a loaf or two hidden away behind the counter for islanders like yourselves," Mrs. O'Connor answered.

"And could we also get a gingerbread man—"

"Or two!" Beth added, interrupting me. "And some doughnuts for sure!"

"And a package of fresh buns and sugar cookies and a few butter tarts and—"

"Slow down Samuel!" Mom said. "We'll make sure we get something of everything."

Mrs. O'Connor laughed loudly. "Wait until I tell everybody that Becky Simmons is back . . . oh, I guess it isn't Becky Simmons any more, but I don't know your married name."

Beth and I exchanged a knowing look.

"My married name was Martin, but I don't go by that name anymore. I haven't for years. It's Rebecca Simmons again."

"Oh," Mrs. O'Connor answered, and the way she said the word spoke more than the word itself. "It's always so nice to see islanders who've left come back to visit. There's been more than a few of you pass through these doors in the last few weeks. Seems like the bakery is one of the first stops for many."

"It was our first stop," I agreed, holding up my suitcase for her to see.

"It doesn't need to be your first stop, but I hope it'll be your daily stop. I expect to be seeing you children in here every day while you're staying on the island. Agreed?"

"Sure thing," Beth said and I nodded in agreement.

Beth leaned close to me. "Do you remember the time . . ." she stopped and smiled.

Of course I knew what she was talking about without her needing to finish the sentence. The time Grandpa gave us money and we bought two dozen doughnuts and sat down by the beach and between us ate them . . . every last one.

"Now is there anything else I can add to that order, Becky?"

"I think that pretty well covers it for . . ."

"Maybe a few more doughnuts," Beth said and I laughed along with her.

"Carrot muffins," I added.

"You want carrot muffins?" Beth asked. "Since when did you start to like carrot muffins?"

"I didn't."

"But his grandfather certainly does," Mrs. O'Connor answered. "Let me throw a couple of big ones in the bag, and tell him they're from me."

"Mrs. O'Connor, what was he like the last time you saw him?" Mom asked, turning slightly away from me.

"Right as rain. That was three . . . no, maybe four days ago. Actually I thought it was a bit strange I hadn't seen him since then. I mentioned it to my Herbie, Mr. O'Connor, and he said he'd take a run up to the house if he didn't show his face by tomorrow."

She put the muffins in the bag along with the other

things and handed it over the counter to Mom. Each item was rung into the cash register and Mom handed over a twenty-dollar bill and got back her change.

"I hope you have a pleasant stay on the island, Becky. If there's anything that Mr. O'Connor or I can do to help let me know. Please . . . let us know. At times like these it's important to remember you can count on your friends and neighbours," she said as she placed a hand on my mother's shoulder.

That was nice . . . wait a second . . . what did she mean by "times like these"?

Chapter Three

Nobody spoke as we walked although I think both Mom and I had the same unspoken question: why hadn't Grandpa been seen for the past few days? We walked quickly up the main drag. The speed we were walking, combined with the slope and the sticky bun gumming up my mouth, made it hard to catch my breath. We turned off onto Grandpa's street, which runs perpendicular to the main street. There were now no sidewalks and we walked along the soft shoulder of the road. Sand quickly got into my shoes, and in spite of the situation I couldn't help but smile slightly. Sand had worked its way into all my memories of this place; just like in no time at all little grains would be lodged in every corner of my suitcase, the pockets of all my shorts, all my shoes and every opening of my body from my belly button to my ears. The whole island was hardly more than a gigantic sandbar.

Almost a year after we'd left the island that last time, I put my hand in the pocket of a pair of shorts I hadn't worn since we were last here and found a little pile of sand inside. Mom had already told us we weren't going back that summer. Carefully I turned the pocket inside out and the sand poured out into my hand. I took it and put it in a little tiny bottle. I still had it in the back of my closet where nobody could find it.

As we walked I noticed there had been changes to the street. Before, it had been lined with small, old cottages. A number of these had been replaced by larger, newer houses. Some of them were so big they took up almost all the property and towered over the neighbouring houses, blocking the view and sunlight. In the driveways of a couple of these monster homes sat expensive luxury cars. I couldn't believe that the same people we used to know on the street lived in those new houses with those fancy cars. I wondered what had happened to all the people who used to live in the vanished little cottages. Where had they all gone to?

We passed the first crossroad and I knew Grandpa's house wasn't very far ahead. I scanned the cottages, but none of them seemed right. Maybe it wasn't as close as I remembered.

"It can't be much farther," I said, more to myself than anybody else.

"It isn't," Mom said. "We're there."

"Where?" Beth asked.

"Here," Mom answered, gesturing with her free hand.

"This is it?" Beth sounded confused.

My mouth dropped open as I stared at the cottage. It was so different I would have passed right by it if Mom hadn't pointed it out. I couldn't believe how much it had changed, for the worse, over the past three years.

The front yard was overgrown with weeds and tall grass. One of the shutters hung on a strange angle, only partially attached to the building. The paint was peeling badly and bare wood could be seen staring out through the remaining white paint. It looked abandoned.

"What happened to it?" I asked in astonishment.

My mother was speechless. She just shrugged and shook her head. She looked sad and shocked. This was the house she had grown up in. It was small but it was always so pretty . . . and now . . .

Mom tried to push open the front gate. It barely moved. One of the hinges was broken and the bottom was lodged in sand. We all squeezed through the opening and walked up the cobblestone path that was almost lost under the sand. As we reached the porch I saw that one of the glass panes in the front door was broken and had been replaced by a piece of cardboard taped in its place. A terrible feeling rolled over me. It felt like a cloud blocking out the sun.

Mom knocked on the door. I held my breath and listened and we waited for an answer. There was no sound. She knocked again, this time much harder. Again there was no reply.

"He probably just isn't home," I suggested hopefully.

"I guess we'll just have to wait until he arrives," Beth said.

Unspoken thoughts filled my head. Maybe he was home, but couldn't get the door, or anything else.

Mom turned the knob and the door swung open. Instantly a wave of stench rushed out at us, almost knocking me backwards.

"That's disgusting!" Beth screeched. "It smells like something died!"

We all looked at each other in shock. Was what she said a possibility? Had something . . . or someone . . . died?

Mom put down Beth's bag. "I want you both to stay here."

I opened my mouth to answer but her steely glare closed it again without any words coming out.

"Fine with me," Beth said. "My stomach wouldn't let me go in there even if I wanted."

Mom pushed the door farther open. "Heeellllooo!" she called out and stepped inside. She disappeared into the dark hallway.

I looked over at Beth. Her face reflected my fears. I dropped my bag to the porch.

"She shouldn't be in there by herself," I said.

"You're not thinking of going in are you?"

"Not thinking . . . doing." I stepped inside before either of us had a chance to talk me out of it. The smell that had seeped through the open door was only a diluted version of what awaited me just inside the house. I wished I'd taken a bigger breath of air before I'd entered.

The door hadn't even closed behind me when Beth jumped in as well and grabbed my arm. "You're not going anywhere . . . without me."

"But the smell, and your stomach?"

"I'll survive," she gagged.

I nodded and took a step forward. Beth was still holding onto my arm.

"Mom!" I called out and took a few more tentative steps down the darkened hall, my sister trailing behind me.

"AAAHHH!" Beth screamed and jumped into the air, digging her fingernails into my arm and making me jump and yell as well.

"What's wrong? What's wrong?" I screamed. All sorts of terrible thoughts flooded through my mind.

"Something brushed past me . . . I think it was a rat! A giant rat!"

A light flashed on and I was momentarily stunned by the brightness.

Mom was standing at the end of the hall, her hand on a light switch. "Not a rat, a cat," Mom said as she pointed to a large cat slinking along the wall.

"A cat? I didn't know Grandpa had a cat," I said.

"He doesn't have *a* cat. He has a *bunch* of cats. I've seen at least five. That's what the smell is," Mom answered. "Watch where you step."

I looked around. There was an overflowing kitty

litter box just inside the door and another equally disgusting one peeking around the corner of the living room up ahead.

"Is Grandpa . . . is he . . . ?" I asked.

"He isn't here."

I felt a weight lift off my shoulders. Of course he wasn't here . . . it had been stupid to think anything else. Why was it I could always think of the worst possible thing that could happen in any situation?

Mom retreated into the darkened living room and we followed after her.

A rush of light accompanied the sound of a blind opening up. Mom walked to a second and then a third window, opening their blinds too, and the room became as bright as outside.

"What . . . what happened here?" I asked in amazement as my eyes scanned the room.

The entire room was filled to overflowing with stacks of newspapers, half-filled glasses and plates of partially eaten food piled high on the tables. Thick dust coated the pictures and knick-knacks, spider webs filled the corners, and grime and dirt streaked the windows. The inside of the house was as bad as the outside.

From where I stood I saw two more kitty litter boxes. Even worse than either the smell or the awful sight of the packed boxes was the "taste" of them. There were grains of grit and sand in my mouth and nose. I could see them in the beams of sunlight streaming in through the windows, suspended in the air. Maybe I was just imagining it, but it was like I could feel the little bits of grit lining my tongue. How could this have happened?

"This is disgusting!" Beth said, covering her mouth with her hand. "I can't stand being here. I've got to leave!" She ran down the hall, the sound of her gagging audible until the slamming of the door marked her exit from the house.

"What happened, Mom? Why is it like this?" I asked.

She shook her head and the expression on her face showed her complete confusion. She looked like she was on the verge of tears and was fighting to hold them inside. Poor Mom.

"I just don't know . . . it's even worse than I could have imagined . . . we have to get some air in here. Can you try to get those windows open while I try to open the ones in the bedrooms? We have to air this place out . . . we have to."

Mom left the room, leaving me alone with the cats. I started counting them. There were certainly more than the five Mom had suggested. There were three curled up on different chairs, totally ignoring me, two more stretching out and staring at the newcomers, the one I'd seen in the hall, and another scratching up a cloud of dust in one of the litter boxes. What was Grandpa doing with all these cats?

I climbed on the couch to reach one of the windows. The couch released a puff of dust in reaction to my step. The window latch was broken, so it couldn't lock. I put both hands on the edge of the glass and pushed up with all my might. It wouldn't budge. It looked to be solidly sealed with dirt and grease. I took my fist and banged the frame hard, at both the top and bottom corners. The glass rattled ominously. I placed my hands back against the frame, braced my legs on the couch and pushed. With a groan it slid up and I was instantly rewarded by a gust of fresh, clean sea air. I pressed my face close to the screen and inhaled deeply.

Refreshed, I bounced off the couch and went to the second window. Its lock was broken as well. I readied myself and put my full muscle into the window. Unexpectedly it flew up and whacked into the top of the sill and I almost fell through the screen.

Some of the papers that were stacked everywhere in the room started to flap and blow in the breeze. A couple were dancing around the room and I chased after them, catching one under my foot and then another with my hands. I put them back in the pile they'd come from. I needed something to weigh them down, so I grabbed a cup off the coffee table. I looked into the cup but couldn't identify what liquid it had been before it had hardened into a disgusting, thick brown crust. I put it down on top of the papers and then wiped my hand against my pants.

My eye was caught by the pictures that lined the mantle. They were all coated with a thick layer of dust . . . all except one. I picked it up. It was a picture of Grandpa and Mom, and Beth and me. Everybody was smiling and looked so happy. It was taken the last summer we were here . . . maybe only a few days before the fight.

"That's better," Mom said as she returned to the room.

I put the picture back down nervously, like I'd been caught doing something wrong.

"A little bit better. What do you want me to do now?" I asked.

"I just don't know what to say, or where to begin," she muttered.

"Is it all like this? I mean, like, are the other rooms this bad?"

"Worse. The kitchen is just awful. And for some reason the phone's not working. I don't know how he could live like this and I don't think we can stay here until it's cleaned up."

"Do you want me to get Beth? She might be better with the breeze and everything. I could start in the kitchen and maybe she could—"

"Get her and then you can both get changed."

"Sure. We'll get into some old clothes and—"

"I was thinking you two could get into your bathing suits. I want you to go down to the beach and have a swim."

"We can't just go and leave you here," I protested. "You need our help."

She shook her head. "The two of you should go for a swim. What I need is to be alone for a while . . . to work."

I could see how hard she was fighting back the tears she didn't want us to see.

Chapter Four

"This is too weird," Beth said as we left the cottage. "I can't even imagine Mom not wanting us to help her clean up."

"I think she just wanted us to have a swim is all," I answered, not saying that I figured Mom needed to be alone with her thoughts more than she needed our help. It was strange seeing Mom on the verge of tears. She always tried so much to be in control. And anybody who knew her—people at her work or her students or neighbours or even family—thought she was always in control, that she was so strong and capable. But I knew better. I could see the times things started to slip away, like when she and Beth had a fight and then she'd leave the room or turn away. She tried to hide it, stay strong. But I knew she wasn't as strong as she pretended.

"Come on, get real. When has Mom ever wanted us to have fun before all our work was done?" Beth asked.

"I guess she just wants us to enjoy our vacation," I suggested.

I wasn't going to admit it, but of course my sister was right. We seemed to do more around the house and have more "responsibilities" than anybody else either of us knew. Mom said that was the way she was raised and the way she thought it was best to raise her children. Mom's mother died when she was little and it was just her and Grandpa. She said she had to do a lot around the house to keep things running, and she wanted us to be able to take care of ourselves too, like she had had to take care of herself, because you never knew what might happen. I hated when she talked like that. It wasn't that I minded doing my share of the work. I just didn't like to think about all the things that could go wrong that would force us to take care of ourselves.

Mom was always going on about how there were "no free lunches" in life, and how you had to "work for what you got." She didn't believe in luck or lottery tickets or wishing for things. If you wanted it you had to work for it. Plain and simple. As far as she was concerned, you had to put your nose to the grindstone and work as hard as you could. That was the way, and the only way, to get things in life.

"I don't know how anybody could live in that house," Beth said.

"It'll be much better by the time we get back," I answered as we walked down the sandy street.

"I don't care how much better it is, I'm not sleeping in that dump tonight."

"Where do you think you're going to sleep?" I asked.

"I don't know, but not in there. And where did all those cats come from?"

I shook my head. "I'm not sure, but there sure are a lot of them."

"I counted nine," Beth replied.

"I only saw eight, but there were a couple out in the yard and I wondered if they belong to Grandpa too."

"HEY!"

Beth and I turned around. A boy a bit older than me, and maybe a little younger than Beth, was riding toward us on his bike. He skidded to a stop right in front of us.

"I saw you two coming out of Mr. Simmons' place," he said.

"Yeah, he's our grandfather," Beth answered. "Not that it's any of your business."

A smile came to the kid's face. "That must mean you're Sam, and you're Beth."

Beth and I exchanged looks.

"You don't remember me, do you?" the kid asked.

I shook my head.

"Buzz?" Beth asked.

Again he smiled. "You do remember," the boy said.

Along with the name came some memories. He lived a dozen houses down from Grandpa and we used to spend time with him when we visited. He was Beth's age, but I was the one who had played with him. We were friends—good friends. He and Beth really, really didn't like each other. Beth called him "Buzz off" and they took turns making fun of each other.

He certainly looked different, and not just older—his hair was long and dangly and not the buzz cut I remembered him having.

"How long has it been?" he asked.

"We haven't been here for three summers," I said.

"I thought it was about that long. Boy, you look different," he said to Beth.

She looked confused.

"You know, all grown up and everything," Buzz continued.

She smiled.

All grown up? Since when is thirteen all grown up? I thought.

"How long are you staying for?" he asked.

"We don't know. Until the day before yesterday we didn't even know we were coming. I don't even think our Grandpa knows we're on the island yet," Beth replied.

"He isn't home. Do you know where he might be?" I asked.

"Could be anywhere. He doesn't exactly keep a schedule or nothing. Just sort of goes where and when he wants."

"Have you seen him lately?" I questioned.

"Yesterday. I brought him up some groceries and a couple of bags of kitty litter."

"And were you talking to him?" Beth asked.

"For a bit."

"Did he seem, you know, okay?" I questioned.

"No different from other times."

"That's good."

"But you have to remember it's always hard to tell with him. Your grandfather is a different sort of guy."

"What do you mean?" I asked, although I thought I knew the answer.

"Don't get me wrong. I like him . . . a lot. It's just that sometimes he's a little bit different. You know, like with those cats. But most of the time I figure he's just cool is all."

I thought Buzz had summed it up pretty well. Grandpa was different from anybody else I had ever met. He was sort of like a big, old, wrinkled kid. He was just as likely to go out and fly a kite or launch a rocket or build a model as he was to do anything serious or adult-like. He threw himself into whatever interested him with his complete and total energy. More than once, at least before she stopped talking about him completely, Mom had mentioned how hard it was being in charge of her father when she was growing up. She'd said that sometimes she felt like she was the parent and he was the kid. I could see that . . . from both of them. I didn't know if he'd ever grown up, or that she wasn't born all grown up.

"We're going to the beach. Do you want to come?" Beth asked.

That was a good idea, but why was she asking "Buzz off" to come anywhere with us? She used to think the whole island wasn't big enough for the two of them.

"Naah. Maybe later. Too many tourists there this time of day."

Beth looked disappointed. "Maybe later?"

"Or maybe you two can come with me," Buzz suggested.

"Where are you going?" Beth asked.

"Out to the Money Pit."

"The Money Pit? Why are you going there?" I asked.

"To watch what's going on."

"I've been out there dozens of times with Grandpa and nothing is ever going on," I said.

"That's right, you've been gone for a while. They're trying to find the treasure again!" Buzz exclaimed.

"Wow, they're going into the pit. That would be amazing to see," I admitted.

"They're using all sorts of heavy digging machinery. Some of those machines are so big they had to hire a special ship to bring them over to the island! So, do you want to come?"

Beth nodded her head enthusiastically. I didn't remember Beth ever being interested in anything Buzz had to say.

"I don't know if we should go," I objected, although it sounded amazing.

"Why not?" Beth asked.

"Mom thinks we're going swimming. She wouldn't be too happy if we just took off someplace else."

"And little Sammy wouldn't want to make his Mommy mad now would he?" Beth chided.

"Shut up! Maybe I just want to go swimming!"

"But isn't there swimming by the pit too?" Beth inquired.

"Yeah, there's a nice spot to swim on Smith's Cove, just down the beach from where they're working," Buzz said.

So much for that idea. "But it's a long way."

"Not too far. We can get there in thirty minutes if we bike it," Buzz said.

"But we don't have bikes," I replied.

"I can loan you each one, no problem."

"You have extra bikes?" I asked.

"Lots. They're just piled in my garage. Every bike that ever belonged to any of my brothers and sisters is there. Some of them are pretty useless but there's a few that are more or less in one piece."

"Won't they mind if we just take their bikes?" Beth questioned.

"I can't see why they would. The next youngest in my family are sixteen and seventeen and they think they're too cool to ride bikes anymore. In fact, only five of my brothers and sisters even live on the island anymore."

"Only five of them?" I asked.

"Yeah, the others have all moved to the mainland, although it seems like all summer long we have one or two of them staying with us, along with their partners, kids, friends and dogs," Buzz explained.

I remembered that Buzz came from a big family but I couldn't remember how big it was.

"How many brothers and sisters do you have?"

"Eight sisters and three brothers."

"Wow, that's incredible!" I exclaimed.

"And I'm the baby. Do you know what that means?" Buzz asked.

I shook my head.

"Almost everything I wear, own, ride, touch, taste or do has already been done by at least somebody else in my family."

"I've never known anybody with that many kids," I said.

Buzz chuckled. "My mom is from Newfoundland. She says you have to have at least ten kids before it's even considered a *middle*-sized family."

"That must have been something, living in a house with that many kids."

"We weren't all there at once. Like I said, I'm the baby. The next youngest is my brother Bobby and he's sixteen. By the time I was born the oldest four had already moved out. Now if I could only convince them to stay out. Come on and we'll get some bikes. You two can keep them for as long as you're on the island."

Buzz walked his bike and we walked along beside him. We approached his house, which was only a dozen doors down from Grandpa's place. It certainly didn't look that much different in size from his—that meant three bedrooms, a little storage room and one bathroom. I couldn't imagine how that many kids could be raised in that small a space.

"Do you have more than one bathroom?" I asked as we neared his house.

"Just the one. And me with eight sisters. It was a nightmare."

The major difference between Buzz's house and my Grandpa's was the way it was maintained. Buzz's place looked like I remembered Grandpa's. It had a coat of bright fresh paint and flowers blooming along the sides of a green, green lawn.

Buzz dropped his bike onto the path. "The bikes are in here," he said as he swung open the doors of a large metal tool shed.

I could see the outlines of at least a dozen bikes inside. Buzz began pulling them out. Some of them were jammed together and the spokes and pedals of the different bikes were all tangled up. The first two bikes he removed were just pieces of junk. One was missing a wheel and the second had neither seat nor pedals. Buzz tossed them to the side.

"Ah, here. This one's better," Buzz announced as he pulled the third free of the tangle.

It was a girl's bike, missing the top bar. It looked old but all the pieces were there. I checked the tires and they were solid.

"This one's okay for you," I said to Beth.

"Why do I have to have a girl's bike?"

"'Cause you're a girl," I shot back.

"And because that's mostly what we have," Buzz added. "Eight sisters, remember?"

"So stop complaining, Beth."

"And here's yours," Buzz said, pulling out another bike.

"Mine? But it's a girl's bike too!"

"Like I said, that's mostly what I got."

"You must have something. Let me have a look," I said as I stepped past him into the shed.

I pulled and prodded the remaining bikes. There were two other boys' bikes but they were in bad shape. The only remaining bikes were all the wrong kind. Reluctantly, I retreated out of the shed.

"Let's saddle up and get going," Buzz said. "The Money Pit awaits."

Chapter Five

We started off down the road. Buzz led, Beth was behind him and I was in the rear. I felt pretty stupid riding a rusty old girl's bike. At least I could be grateful that there wasn't anybody from my school on the island. There were some kids at my school who gave me a hard time because I wasn't so great at sports. Bad enough that they said I threw a ball like a girl without people seeing me riding a bike like a girl.

A car whizzed by, followed almost immediately by a pick-up truck. The truck passed so fast and so close to us that the gust of hot wind almost pushed me off the edge of the road and onto the sandy shoulder.

"Do I just remember wrong or is there a lot more traffic on the island than before?" I asked.

"A lot more," Buzz called out over his shoulder.

"Cars and trucks and boats and swimmers and people in the stores. My mom says it's like living in . . ."

Another car with its radio blaring, pulling a boat behind it, zoomed by and the last part of his sentence was lost.

"Like living in the city," he continued.

"Nothing wrong with the city," Beth added.

"Nothing if that's where you want to live," Buzz said. "But that's not where most of us who are out here on the island want to live."

"If people don't like all the changes why do they let them do it? Why don't they stop them from coming to the island?" I asked.

"Free country. Besides, some people are happy about all the extra bodies."

"Like who?"

"The people running stores and doing construction on the new houses and renting out boats think it's great. More people means more money," Buzz explained.

Beth rode up beside Buzz. "Was that a satellite dish on your house?" she asked, completely changing the subject.

"Yeah, we got it last year."

"So you can get television? Like regular stuff and everything?" Beth questioned.

"Everything. We have the movie channel, the sports network, MTV—"

"That's fantastic!" Beth exclaimed.

"That's one of the changes I like," Buzz admitted. "Your Grandpa doesn't have a dish does he?"

"Are you kidding? He doesn't even have a TV," I answered. It was one of the few drawbacks to our summers here. No Saturday morning cartoons or baseball on the tube, or reruns of my favourite shows.

"The MTV video awards are on tonight," Buzz said.

"Yeah I know. I was going to watch them with my . . . with my friend," Beth answered.

"Your friend? I thought it was Brent who . . ." I began.

"Brent was coming over and he is my friend or I wouldn't have invited him to our house."

"But I thought he was . . ." I started to say when the hot glare from Beth's eyes caused the words to melt right out of my mouth. Why didn't she want me to mention that Brent was her boyfriend? She usually missed no opportunity to mention him. Did she think if she told Buzz that somehow it might get back to Mom?

"Do you two want to come over tonight and watch the awards at my place?" Buzz asked.

"Yeah, I'd love . . . I mean that would be good," Beth answered.

"Video awards? I'll take a pass on that one," I replied.

Buzz started chattering away about some music video they both liked and I tuned them out. My mind turned instead to the Money Pit.

I remember Grandpa telling me stories about the Money Pit from as long ago as I can remember anything. I knew it so well that it was like a movie in my head, and I could hear Grandpa's words and see the things he described. It was one of the greatest mysteries of the world and it had been unsolved for over two hundred years.

It all began back in 1795 when a couple of kids who lived on the island first found a spot in the ground that looked like somebody had been digging. Right above the depression there was a tree with sawed-off branches that looked like it had had ropes or a pulley attached to it. The sorts of things you'd use to lower something heavy into the ground.

I pictured in my mind the first time I heard the story. Grandpa had taken me to the very spot where the Money Pit was located. We sat there as the sun went down and he told me all about Captain Kidd the pirate and how it was his treasure buried underneath our very feet. It still sent a shiver up my spine, thinking back to that night, sitting under the stars, hearing the tale.

And my Grandpa described to me what those two kids did next—exactly what I would have done. They got shovels and started to dig. He said they just got down a few feet when they hit something solid. They started to clear away the shifting sand and found large, flat flagstones, ten feet across altogether. Somebody had gone to a lot of work to bring those stones up from the water's edge.

I could hear Grandpa's words in my ears, the excitement in his voice, and feel the tingle of little pinpricks in the back of my head as he told the story.

And at that point, Grandpa stopped the story and

stood up and walked the few dozen feet to his parked pick-up truck. He reached into the back and took out a lantern and two shovels, then brought them over to me. He lit the lantern, set it down in the sand and, right there and then, we started to dig. We must have dug for three hours, me thinking we'd find the treasure and him knowing we wouldn't, but enjoying it just the same.

Of course, those boys didn't find any treasure, either. They dug down through layer after layer of sand, finding each ten-foot level marked by more flat stones or even a barrier of logs, stopping them from digging deeper. But they persisted, positive that nobody would have ever gone to this much trouble unless there was something really valuable down there. The way Grandpa told it, those boys eventually dug down almost thirty feet, using the beams they'd uncovered as side supports to stop the whole thing from caving in and burying them alive. In the end, they had to give up.

But while they were stopped from digging deeper by the sand, nothing stopped the story from being spread far and wide, and more and more people came to carry on the digging. Over the next two hundred years a dozen groups came and left. Each group got farther and deeper: forty, fifty, sixty feet. At each ten-foot interval they came across another layer of wood or clay or stone. And with each layer the work became harder, but every group of diggers was even more certain than the last;

somebody had gone to tremendous effort to hide something, and whatever was hidden must be immensely valuable.

A car's horn blared and I was jolted out of my thoughts, turning to the side of the pavement so sharply that I almost fell off my bike as the vehicle sped by, hitting me with the wave of hot air it pushed in front of it.

"IDIOT!" Buzz yelled and shook his fist at the driver.

Maybe I had drifted too far out toward the centre. I'd have to keep at least part of my mind on the traffic. A massive lumber truck barrelled toward us on the opposite side of the road. As it passed, another gust of hot air blew past, carrying with it a gritty hail that stung my face. I swerved off to the side before I regained my balance.

Buzz pulled his bike to a stop and Beth and I came to rest on either side of him.

"There it is," he said.

"Where?" I asked.

"Behind those walls."

I looked up ahead and off to the side where he was pointing. There were brightly painted, solid metal fences extending into the distance.

"I don't remember there being a fence around the pit," Beth said.

"Yeah, Grandpa always took us right there. Once we even spent a time digging. We didn't find any treasure or anything but we did find a piece of wood. He said it was from one of the layers that had been dug up," I commented.

"They put it up when they started digging this time," Buzz said.

"But that would stop people from seeing," I reasoned.

"That's the idea. They want it all private."

"But . . . if we can't see . . . why did we come out?" I asked.

"Well, you can't see through the fences. But they're just built on sand. We'll stash the bikes and dig under. Then we'll sneak up close enough to have a good look."

"Is that a good idea? Won't we get in trouble?" I asked anxiously.

"Of course not. I do it all the time."

"And you haven't got in trouble?"

"Naaah . . . of course they've never caught me . . . not yet, anyway."

Chapter Six

We rode along a little bit farther until we came to the place where the road ran closest to the fence. Buzz jumped off his bike and Beth and I did the same thing. We walked the bikes toward the fence. There was no point in even trying to ride through the sand. Pushing the bike was hard enough, since the wheels dug in deeply and skittered off to the side.

"Let's stash them here," Buzz said, dropping his bike between a couple of the few bushes that grew among the shifting sand and sparse grass.

We walked the rest of the way to the fence. It was painted bright yellow and was made of corrugated metal. It extended well above my head. Even if I jumped up I couldn't touch the top, let alone see over it. White signs were spaced out along the fence. They read, "*Danger! No Trespassing! Heavy equipment and excavation!*"

"I understand all of it except the last word. What does excavation mean?" I asked.

"Digging," Beth answered.

"Big-time digging. You'll see," Buzz added.

"Maybe we shouldn't go," I said.

"Don't be scared little Sammy," Beth taunted.

"It does say danger, you know," I responded.

"It's only dangerous if we get too close, and believe me, we won't get that close," Buzz said reassuringly. "Okay?"

"I guess so."

"You two should leave your knapsacks here. What's in them, anyway?"

"Towels, some sandwiches, a couple of water bottles."

"And I brought along a deck of cards as well," I said.

"Cards? Were you going to play cards at the beach?" Buzz asked.

"Not play—" I started to say.

"Don't get him started," Beth snapped. "I'm warning you!"

I shot her a dirty look. "I use them to perform magic tricks."

"You can do magic?"

"Some. Do you want to see a good trick?" I asked.

"Sure," Buzz answered enthusiastically.

"Then you're out of luck because Sam only has bad tricks," Beth said.

"Shut up, Beth!"

"Don't tell me to shut up you little—"

"Hold on a second," Buzz interrupted. "Let him show me the trick and I'll decide if it's stupid."

"Why are we wasting our time here with his tricks? Let's get in and see the Money Pit," Beth said.

"No rush. It's not like the pit is going anywhere," Buzz said. "It's been there for two hundred years. I figure it'll wait five more minutes. Besides, I like card tricks."

Beth made a face and sulked off. She sat down about two dozen feet away, looking away from where we sat.

I pulled off my knapsack and undid the buckle. I grabbed the water bottle from the top of the pack, took a long slug of water and offered it to Buzz. As I got out the deck of cards he took an equally big drink. I took the cards out of the package and shuffled them noisily. My hands felt a little shaky. I knew it wasn't because I wasn't sure about whether or not I could do the trick, but because I was feeling nervous about going in the pit area. What if we got caught? What would Mom think?

Buzz settled into the sand under the thin band of shade provided by the fence.

"Cut the cards . . . as many times as you want," I said.

"If I had a chain saw I'd cut the cards and good," Beth chimed in.

"Please ignore the heckling from the crowd," I responded.

I couldn't help but notice that Beth seemed even

more difficult than usual. It was almost like she was mad that Buzz was paying attention to me instead of her.

Buzz cut the cards and went to hand them back to me.

"No, I don't want to touch them. Please place the deck of cards right here in my shirt pocket," I said, using one hand to open the pocket.

Buzz dropped the cards in.

"Now pick a number from ten to fifteen."

"Um . . . eleven," Buzz said.

I pulled out eleven cards and placed them face down on the sandy ground.

"What would be the best hand a person could have in poker?" I asked.

"I don't know," Buzz hesitated. "Maybe kings or aces I guess."

"Aces would certainly be higher than kings. How about four aces?"

"Yeah I guess so," he agreed. "That would be a good hand."

"Good. There are four aces among these eleven cards."

"How do you know that?"

"Because I can see right through the cards. It's all part of my special magic powers," I answered.

"Yeah, right," Beth muttered, still not looking, but obviously listening to what was going on. "You have as much power as a dead battery."

I ignored her. I'd had even more practice ignoring her than I had doing magic.

"I'll prove my powers."

Slowly, I held my hand above each card and closed my eyes. I stopped over the second card and then turned it over. It was the ace of hearts.

"Good guess," Buzz said.

I continued over the third and then stopped at the fourth card. I flipped this fourth one over and it was the ace of diamonds. Before he could respond I also flipped over the fifth card, revealing the ace of spades.

"Still think I'm guessing?" I asked.

"The cards must be marked," Buzz replied.

"Think so? Then why don't you figure out how they're marked and flip over the last ace. It's under one of the six remaining cards."

Buzz bent over intently, staring at each of the cards in turn. He went back over them all a second time. Finally he stopped over one of the cards and flipped it. It was the four of clubs.

"Why did you pick that one?" I asked.

"It's a little bit bent and I thought that was how you were telling the aces."

"How about this one? It's not bent. Do you think it could be the ace?" I asked, knowing full well it wasn't.

"I don't know," he said.

"You would if you could see through cards. It isn't this one. The fourth ace is right here," I said flipping over another card.

"How did you do that?"

"I told you . . . magic."

Buzz chuckled. "I don't know how you did it . . . but I'm impressed. Can you show me some other tricks later on?"

I smiled and nodded enthusiastically. I could show him another fifty tricks and most of them were a lot better than this one, but they involved more setting up of the deck or using one of my special decks of cards.

"Can we get going now?" Beth demanded. "I've already seen the amazing nerdo perform his tricks. I want to see what's on the other side of the fence."

Buzz turned around, dropped to his knees and began scooping away handfuls of sand from the base of the fence. Beth put her knapsack over by the bikes and then dropped down beside Buzz and started digging as well. Reluctantly I did the same. The sand was loose and easy to move, but it just as easily slid back down the side of the hole we were digging and partially refilled it. I could imagine how hard it would have been to dig a deep hole like the Money Pit. How could anybody possibly do it?

"I thought you'd done this before," Beth said to Buzz.

"I have."

"Then why didn't we just go through one of the holes you dug before?"

"We are . . . sort of. . . I guess," Buzz answered. "I always go in around here."

"And you fill the hole back in every time?" she asked.

"I don't have to. The sand is so fine and the wind is so strong it just gets filled in all by itself."

We had to make the hole wider and wider to stop the sides from collapsing. Within a few minutes we reached the bottom edge of the fence. Buzz reached underneath and started pulling out sand from the other side.

"Hey, watch it!" I called out as a handful of sand sprayed into my face. I spat out the grains that had found their way into my mouth.

"Sorry, it was an accident," Beth replied.

If it was an accident how come she had a little smile on her face? I picked up a handful of sand. If I had more nerve I would have "accidentally" tossed it at her.

The three of us kept on digging until we made the hole deep enough for us to fit through. I sat back to rest for a moment—then looked over in time to see Buzz's legs squirming under the fence and then disappear. I lowered my head down after him. He was standing on the other side. I "swam" under and joined him. Beth followed behind, pushing her head through the hole and then dragging her body after us. Soon she was standing beside us.

"Yuck, I've got sand all over my hair," Beth said as she shook her head. "My hair must look awful!"

"No, it looks fine," Buzz said.

She stopped shaking and smiled. "Thanks," she said. "But it can look a lot better than this, especially after a good sham—"

"Does this look like a shampoo commercial?" I asked. "Can we go to the pit?"

Buzz chuckled. "Come on, it's this way."

Beth and I trailed behind him. We followed him up the side of a large sand dune. The sand streamed down as we climbed up and I dropped down to use my hands to help get more traction. Buzz plopped down at the very top of the dune and I dropped down beside him.

"Wow," was all I could think to say as my eyes opened wide at the sight before me.

Chapter Seven

"This is unbelievable," I said, more to myself than to the others.

"It really is something," Buzz agreed.

"I don't understand. Is that the Money Pit?" Beth asked.

Beth was referring to an enormous hole in the ground. I couldn't tell just how big it was because we still weren't that close, but it was gigantic. The last time I'd been here it was nothing more than a wide, flat, sandy plain.

"That's how they're getting to the treasure," Buzz explained. "Rather than just dig straight down the shaft of the pit, the way the other expeditions have tried, they're digging an enormous hole. The Money Pit is right in the centre of that hole."

"How big is it?" I asked.

"Over a hundred feet across at the very top and then it gets narrower as they dig down. By the time they reach the treasure it probably won't be very wide. Maybe not much wider than the original shaft."

"But even if it's wider they still must have problems with the sand collapsing into it," I suggested.

"Nope," Buzz said. "Do you see that smokestack?"

How could I miss it? Thick black smoke rose up into the sky.

"That's the asphalt factory," Buzz explained.

"Asphalt? Like they use in roads and stuff?" I asked.

"Exactly the same."

"But why do they need that?"

"They're using the asphalt to line the sides so it doesn't keep collapsing."

"Like it did even when we were digging under the fence," Beth commented.

"Exactly. That's always been one of the biggest problems. The deeper they get the worse it becomes," Buzz agreed.

"But that's not the biggest problem. What about the flooding?" I asked.

"Flooding isn't a problem at all for them."

"But flooding has been a major problem since an expedition unplugged that underground passage," I said.

"What underground passage?" Beth asked.

"Didn't you listen to any of Grandpa's stories at all?" I questioned.

"Some. What underground passage?"

"It leads in from the bay," Buzz said. "It enters the Money Pit about forty feet down and floods the whole bottom. No matter how hard they tried to pump it out the whole bottom stayed filled with water."

"But how can that . . ." I started to ask before I looked out toward the bay and was stopped by the sight. Stretching across the whole shallow end of the cove was a white wall of concrete. Behind it the sea rippled, but on this side was only mud. They'd dammed off the entire cove! No water could flood the pit from the underground passage because they'd stopped it from entering the passage!

"Some water still gets in, you know, because it's an island and they're digging deep, but it's all taken care of by the pumps. One set takes water out of the pit and a second set keeps on draining the part of the cove they dammed off."

"How do you know so much about it?" Beth asked.

"Probably been talking to the guys who worked here," I answered for him.

"That doesn't work. I've tried to talk to a couple of them, guys me and my family know, but they wouldn't tell me anything. Nobody's talking. They're not allowed to say anything to anybody. They're not even allowed to tell people that they work here."

"What do you mean, like they had to 'cross their hearts and promise not to tell'?" I laughed.

"Sort of," Buzz answered and I stopped laughing. "They signed some papers and if they get caught talking about it they can be fired."

"So if nobody would talk to you how do you know so much?"

"This is the most exciting thing happening on the island, so I've spent a lot of time watching."

"I don't see how that would help. I can hardly see anything from here," I said, cupping one hand above my eyes to cut the glare from the sun. The pit and all the other stuff, trucks and big diggers and earth-moving equipment, was still a long way off.

"Who said anything about here? We're going to get closer . . . a lot closer."

How much closer did he have in mind? My desire to *see* was weaker than my fear of being *seen*. Before I could even think to object, Buzz had started to scramble down the front of the dune. He stopped halfway down and took refuge behind a large rock. He motioned for us to follow. Beth followed without hesitating and I was left with no choice but to join them. Even though the equipment and the men were still far away I felt awfully exposed as I slid down the side of the dune. Before I even reached them they were off again, then they waited at the bottom of a little gully between the first dune and a second, smaller one that rose up in front. I started down and tripped. I slammed face first into the sand, somer-saulted twice and came to a sudden stop as I crashed into Buzz. He offered me a hand and helped me up.

"Finally, you perform a good trick!" Beth laughed.

I shook my head to dislodge some sand and pulled my T-shirt out of my bathing suit to free up the sand that had lodged there as well. At least I'd kept my mouth shut and didn't have to spit any out.

"We have two choices. Do you want to see the pit or the dam?" Buzz asked.

"Um . . . which one's closer?" I asked, although what I was really wondering was which one was safer. That would determine my choice.

"They're about the same distance. The dam is that way," he said, gesturing to the left, "and the pit is that way," he said, pointing to the right.

"Let's go to the dam," I suggested.

"The dam?" Beth asked. "You'd rather see the dam than the Money Pit?"

"I just thought it would be interesting." What I really meant was that it would probably have fewer people and less activity so there'd be less chance of us being caught.

"It's pretty cool, but I've got to warn you, it's harder to get to than the pit. It's so open—there aren't many places to hide."

I swallowed hard. What an idiot I was.

"Maybe we better do the pit," Beth suggested.

I worked hard not to smile. I was trying to think of the last time my sister ever said anything that made my life happier or easier. My memory wasn't that long.

"The pit it is. Remember to stay low and be careful. And one other thing. If we get separated, or discovered—"

"Discovered?" I interrupted.

"By the people who work there. If we're seen then run like crazy. We'll meet up back at the bikes. Okay?"

We nodded our heads in agreement. The one thing I didn't need was to be reminded to run. If I was seen my legs would work even if my head didn't.

Rounding the side of the second dune, I could see there was a large flat section of ground broken at the end by another high sand dune. The open space was mostly sand, but cutting through the middle was a gravel road. As I watched, a massive dump truck appeared around the side. I ducked down behind some rocks, along with Beth and Buzz.

As the truck neared I was awestruck by its size. It wasn't just the type of dump truck you'd see driving along the road. It was enormous! It was so big it could fit two or three of those regular dump trucks in its massive back. The wheels must have been ten feet high and would have just rolled over the rocks we were hiding behind. The truck roared by, kicking up a thick trail of dust and dirt as it passed, partially obstructing our view. Farther down the road it came to a stop and a loud beeper sound signalled it was backing up. It aimed its backside off the road and the back started to rise up, dumping a load of sand onto an existing pile. The big tailgate slammed shut as the last of the sand emptied out. It lowered its bed and drove off slowly, finally disappearing around the far side of the big dune.

"That was the biggest truck I ever saw in my life," I said.

"Yeah, they're special trucks for sand quarries and construction sites. They can't drive on roads because they're so large they'd take up two lanes and they're so heavy they'd break the pavement," Buzz said.

"They're using them to take away all the sand they dig from the pit. This is where it's being piled."

Where the truck had dumped its load was a series of sandy "hills" extending along the gravel road. Judging by all the sand they'd dumped, they must have dug deep already.

"Let's go before the next truck comes," Buzz said. He bounded away and was half the distance to the gravel road before Beth and I took to our feet. As I moved I kept my head slightly turned to where the next truck might appear at any second. There was absolutely no place to hide, and if a truck did round the corner, the driver couldn't help but see us.

I doubled my pace and quickly closed the distance between me and Buzz. Beth fell behind and yelled out for me to slow down. That was the last thing on my mind. All I wanted was to get to those piles of sand which were the first available place to hide. I was actually amazed at just how fast I was moving. Maybe I wasn't that great at running when I was chasing a soccer ball, but I guess I could really run when I was fuelled by fear. I pulled up even with Buzz and then moved ahead of him.

Beth had just caught up to us at the piles of sand when the loud roar of an engine filled the air. We all looked toward the sound and saw another big dump truck, smoke billowing out of its stacks, come rumbling around the corner. We scrambled for cover between the piles.

"Keep low," Buzz said, as he threw himself against the back of the large pile of sand.

Keep low . . . I would have buried myself in the sand if I thought it would help. The noise of the engine got louder and louder . . . it was unbelievably loud. The closest thing I could think of was the time I'd stood beside railroad tracks to watch a train pass by. I pressed myself lower into the pile of sand. I could actually feel the truck vibrating up through the sand and into my body.

The truck passed out of sight, blocked by the pile we were hidden behind. That was okay with me. I figured if I couldn't see something as big as that truck there was no way the driver could see something as small as us.

The rumbling and roar were joined by a new sound—the sharp, high-pitched beeping of the truck's back-up signal. The sounds got louder and louder. What was happening? I looked up and recoiled in shock as I saw the very top of the sand pile above us start to crumble down and the bright yellow metal of the truck shoot through. It started to rise up . . . the tail gate opened and a mountain of sand started to stream out on top of us!

Chapter Eight

My scream was intertwined with those of Beth and Buzz, and all of our voices were lost beneath the roar of the engine and the sound of the sand sliding out of the truck. In terror I leaped to my feet and tried to run. I stumbled a few feet and staggered, tumbling over onto my face. I shoved myself up on my knees and struggled forward, suddenly aware that I wasn't crawling as much as swimming through a sea of sand that surrounded me. A massive weight pushed against my back and I was overwhelmed and pinned down. The sand still surged all around me and I was struck with the clear thought that I was about to drown to death in the sand. I felt a shocking sense of calm as it flowed over top of me and everything went completely black.

Then I felt something grab my arm and I was

pulled forward, breaking the surface of the sand. I coughed and sputtered badly. Buzz was holding on to my arm and as he dragged me forward I felt the sand digging into my face.

"Sam, are you okay? Are you okay?" Beth screamed.

I coughed and gagged, my heart pounding right through my chest. I looked up at her with blurry, sand-filled eyes. She looked as frantic and scared as I felt. I coughed and then rolled my tongue around in my mouth. My teeth and tongue were coated with sand as well.

"Sam, answer me! Answer me! Are you okay?" she screamed again.

I spat onto the ground, losing the last little bit of moisture left in my mouth, and then nodded to her. I was shaking all over. Beth threw her arms around me and hugged me hard. This shocked and surprised me more than being buried by the sand, and my arms hung limp at my sides. I couldn't believe any of this.

The engine of the truck roared and I turned to see it appear around the side of the sand pile and then roar off. The ground stopped rumbling and the thunder of the engine diminished with each passing second. He'd almost killed me and he hadn't even seen us.

"We're going home . . . right now," Beth announced.

"It's not much farther . . ." Buzz started to say.

"You can do what you want, but I'm taking my brother home."

Beth took me by the arm and started to lead me off. I was so shocked by her actions I didn't even try to argue or fight. Actually, I still felt in an almost dream-like state; none of this could have possibly been real. She led me away like I was a limp balloon at the end of a string. Buzz trailed behind us as we circled around the side of the newly dumped mountain of sand and reached the flat, open plain.

"HEEEYYY!"

All three of us turned to face the voice. Off in the distance were two men—security guards. At their side was a large dog. They started jogging toward us. I felt my stomach tighten up and at the same instant my knees got all loose and weak.

"We're in trouble," Beth said.

"What's going to happen to us?" I asked weakly. I felt like I was going to cry.

"Nothing . . . if they don't catch us," Buzz answered and then sprang away at a dead run. "Come on!" he yelled over his shoulder.

Beth and I hesitated for a split second and then it was like one of those "fight or flight" nature movies you see in school; we ran after Buzz and away from the guards.

Beth was right at my side as we hit the gravel road. Buzz was more than halfway to the safety of the sand dune. I risked a glance over my shoulder . . . they'd let the dog loose! I was terrified! It was much closer to us than the men . . . a big, black blur of furry movement, closing in on us with each stride. I wanted to scream but my lungs were practically empty. He'd be on us in just a few seconds and there was no chance of escape. I imagined his teeth sinking into the back of my leg and being pulled to the ground and . . .

Like a black bullet the dog shot between Beth and me, and we both staggered to the side in surprise. It raced off, chewing up ground with each massive stride. It was running for Buzz! He was just about to disappear around the first dune and would make it before the dog closed the distance. Still, that left him far from the fence and with no place to hide.

At that instant I heard the noise of an engine and looked over. There was a four-wheel-drive land buggy closing in on us from the side. Beth saw it at the same time and we exchanged the same look of hopelessness. We stopped running. There was no point in pretending. We were caught.

I turned around and bent slightly over. My side was hurting, my knees felt like jello, my head was spinning and I struggled to catch my breath. Anxiously, I watched the men coming toward us. What were they going to do to us? They'd slowed down to a fast walk. They were wearing grey uniforms and had thick black belts. From their belts hung those billy clubs that policemen carry. They were both still puffing and out of breath, but that didn't disguise the angry looks on their faces.

The buggy continued to rush toward us from the other side and skidded to a stop just as the two guards reached us.

"What do you two think you're doing!" demanded

one of the guards as he reached out and grabbed me by the arm.

I was so scared I couldn't speak. All I could think about was his iron grip digging into me. I felt my chin start to quiver and fought hard not to cry.

The second guard reached out for Beth.

"Leave us alone!" she burst out as she brushed his hand away from her arm. Thank goodness she was here, she wouldn't let them hurt me.

"We don't have to leave you alone! You're trespassing and you're both in trouble! Big trouble!" he yelled.

The driver jumped from the truck and together the two of them grabbed Beth from both sides. She didn't struggle or argue this time.

"Take them into the back of the buggy," ordered the driver. "We better find out what Bruno did to the third kid."

In my rush of fear I'd forgotten about Buzz. That dog might have torn him to pieces!

They led us away and I was half-lifted into the back of the vehicle. Beth was dumped beside me and the two men climbed in as well. Before they'd even sat down the buggy lurched forward and one of them was almost thrown out the back. He grabbed on to the roof and cursed loudly.

"You have no idea how much trouble you're in," the seated guard said quietly.

I don't know what scared me more, the words or the way he said them, softly and through clenched teeth. They were both still breathing heavily and were drenched in sweat. Maybe we shouldn't have run . . . maybe if we had given ourselves up right away we could have talked to them . . . running probably only made them madder. Why did I even come here? I should have told Buzz and Beth no and insisted that we all stay away. I could have threatened to tell Mom if Beth didn't listen and . . . "mama's boy": I could hear Beth's words in my ears. I hadn't had any choice but to come under the fence.

I looked up and saw one of the guards glaring at me. I looked out the plastic window to escape his gaze. The buggy rocked and bucked and tilted on a strange angle as we partially climbed and partially rounded the sand dune behind which Buzz had disappeared. Buzz! What had happened to him? We slowed down quickly and my back pressed against the cabin of the buggy. It turned sharply and then came to a stop. One of the guards leaped from the back even before it had come to a complete stop.

"Don't even think about running!" the second one snapped, waving a threatening finger at us as he, too, jumped out the back.

There was no danger of that. I wasn't sure my legs would even hold me up if I tried to stand.

"Get him off me! Get him off me!" I heard Buzz's voice scream.

I tried to see him through the plastic but I couldn't see either him or the guards. I strained my neck and pushed against the plastic cover until Buzz came into view. He was lying on the ground, face down, screaming, with the three men surrounding him and the dog perched atop him. The dog must have mauled him badly!

One of the men grabbed the dog by the collar, snapped on a leash and dragged it off Buzz. It snarled and yapped and dug in its heels like it wanted to stay right where it was. The other two grabbed Buzz, one on each arm, and practically lifted him up. He hung there between them, his feet not even touching the ground. I couldn't see any blood or bites.

"In, boy!" yelled a voice.

Before either Beth or I had a chance to react, the dog jumped up into the back of the buggy. Instinctively I drew my hands to my sides and pressed myself away.

"Sit!" the guard ordered.

Just as I was going to answer and tell him we already were sitting, the dog followed his order. It wasn't bad enough that I was scared. Now I felt stupid, too.

"Is . . . is it . . . a friendly dog?" Beth asked hesitantly.

"Yeah, really friendly. That's why we use him as a guard dog," he snarled. He looked even more fierce than the dog itself.

"Let me down!" I heard Buzz yell. He was behind the buggy, framed by its canvas flap. He was still suspended in mid-air between the two men.

"Sure thing, kid!" one of them answered as they threw him into the truck. He landed on the floor with a loud thud and slid into the dog, which growled menacingly.

"Quiet!" the guard ordered.

The dog stopped growling and Buzz scrambled to take a seat beside Beth. He drew up his legs to get as far away as possible from the dog, which was still eyeing him like dinner.

"Are you all right?" Beth asked in a hushed tone.

Buzz nodded. "He just . . . just came up and jumped on me. Knocked me for a loop and then sat on my back, growling."

The two guards chuckled.

"It isn't the dog you should be afraid of."

"What . . . what do you mean?" Buzz asked.

The two guards looked at him and then at each other. They didn't answer. We drove along in silence, while I imagined the worst possible ending to the unanswered question. Unfortunately, I had a very good imagination and all sorts of things popped into my mind.

"Mom's going to kill us," Beth whispered.

"Do your parents know where you are?" one of the guards asked.

"Um . . . no," I stammered.

"And yours?" he asked Beth.

"No . . . he's my brother."

"And are you another brother?"

"No," Buzz answered. "My parents don't know, either."

"Does *anybody* know you were coming out here?" he asked.

"Nobody, I guess," I answered.

"So if you three were late coming home they

wouldn't come here looking for you," the guard said.

"I guess not," I mumbled.

"Interesting," the other guard said. "So if, like, something happened to you and you didn't come home at all then nobody would have even known where to look for you, would they?"

The two guards exchanged a cold, hard look and I felt a chill rise up my spine and lodge itself in my head.

"So if you three were to, like . . . I don't know . . . get caught up in the machinery of the conveyor belt, nobody would even think to come out here looking for you. Nobody would know anything until they found your bodies . . . or what was left of your bodies, all caught up in the machine."

The chill exploded out of my head into every part of my body.

"Yeah, but they'd still discover them and, you know, they might ask questions. Besides, the whole operation would be shut down while they scraped them out of the gears and things. That wouldn't work," the second commented.

"People fall into the ocean all the time. You know, one kid goes swimming and gets caught in a rip tide . . . maybe like the little one there," he said, pointing at me. "And then the other two try to rescue him and all three drown. At least that's what they'd think when they found the remains."

My mouth dropped open. These men were talking about killing us and making it look like an accident! This couldn't be real . . . this was like a bad movie.

"You ever seen a body that drowned?" one asked the other.

"Never. How about you?"

"Once. It gets all bloated and swollen and you can't even recognize who it is. Even their mothers won't be able to identify them. The police have to use dental records to make a positive I.D." He turned to us. "You kids go to the dentist regularly?"

"Um . . . um . . . yeah . . . I've never had any cavities," I muttered, making no sense.

"Oh good, a corpse with perfect teeth!" he laughed.

"That won't matter. With all the sharks around these parts and the tides there's no way they'll ever find the remains."

"You can't just dump us in the ocean," Beth pleaded.

"You can't!" Buzz agreed.

"They're right," the second guard admitted.

I felt a rush of relief. They weren't going to hurt—

"Drowning is too difficult to fake," he continued. "Maybe they could fall into the pit and get smothered."

My brief sense of relief was replaced by total terror. It was only a few minutes before that I'd been saved from that fate and the memory still lingered even more clearly than the sand that had lodged itself into every pore of my body.

"Nah, that won't work. What's the point in burying them when they'll just be dug up again? Besides, with the asphalt they're pouring there really aren't any cave-ins and there'll be too many questions."

"Asphalt! Hey, that gives me an idea!" one guard exclaimed. "What's the temperature of the asphalt furnace?"

"I don't know. Must be pretty hot though. Hot enough to melt rock into liquid," the other acknowledged.

"Hmmmm . . . hot enough to melt rock would make it hot enough to melt other things . . . like bone."

He reached forward and I pressed myself against Beth and away from him. But his hand shot past me and lifted up the flap separating the cab from the back. The driver turned around.

"Take us to the asphalt factory," he said.

Chapter Nine

"That's where I was headed," the driver replied. He must have been listening in on what they were saying . . . and he agreed with their plan.

"Good! Step on it. We don't want to waste any time. We need to get this job done and fast."

He let go of the flap and took his seat again as the vehicle picked up speed and the engine roared louder.

"You can't—" Buzz started to say.

"We can do anything we want, kid!" the guard snarled.

"But, but we were just—" Buzz tried to continue.

"It doesn't matter what you were trying to do. What matters is what *we're* going to do *now*."

Beth started to sniffle and I could feel her shake, although with her legs pressed tightly against mine I wasn't sure if it was her, or me, or both of us. I wanted to say something to comfort her, but there was nothing I could say or do. It was always Beth who was in charge. I felt the truck slow down and then skid to a stop.

"Please, couldn't you just let us go? We'll never come back again, we promise!" Beth pleaded. I could hear the catch in her voice. She was fighting back tears.

"No, we can't just let you go. Get out of the truck," the driver said as both guards jumped off the tail of the buggy. The dog, still on the end of the leash, leaped off as well.

All three of us remained frozen to the seats, unable to move.

"Get off now!" one of them ordered.

Nobody moved.

"Don't make me climb up there and drag you off!" the other threatened.

There was no more point in fighting them now than there had been in running from them before. I stood up on shaky legs and Beth and Buzz followed. As I walked to the end of the truck the driver reached up and offered me a hand down.

"Be careful, the ground is pretty rough here. You might turn an ankle," he said.

What a stupid thing to say! Here he was getting ready to throw us into a furnace and he didn't want me to get hurt. I guess he didn't want to have to carry me if I couldn't walk.

I jumped down without taking his outstretched hand. We were standing in front of a large door on the side of a building. The building was topped with the big smokestack I'd seen from a distance. Thick, black smoke billowed out of it. Anxiously, I looked all around. There had to be somebody who could help us. Nobody else was in sight, although I could hear machinery and voices in the background.

I couldn't help thinking about Mom. She'd never know what had happened to us . . . we didn't even have a chance to say goodbye.

"I'll go and get somebody to take care of things," the driver said as he circled around the side of the buggy. He opened the large sliding door of the building and disappeared inside.

"You can't do this," Buzz said.

"Of course we can, kid. It's our job."

"Your job! It's your job to kill kids who trespass?" Beth asked, tears starting to form in her eyes.

One of the guards started to chuckle and then the other joined him. They tried to stop but they looked at us and the chuckles turned to laughter. One of them was laughing so loud his eyes misted over like he was going to cry. Not only were they mean killers but they were enjoying the thought of ending our lives! How sick could they be?

"Our job isn't to kill children . . . or anybody," the bigger of the two said, fighting back his laughter. "Our job is to keep away trespassers and to turn them over to the police if we find them."

"Then why are you going to kill us?" Buzz implored.

They both started laughing again. This time harder than the first time. This was too insane to be real. Maybe we could run now while they were distracted. If only one of us got away they couldn't kill us. Maybe we didn't have much chance of escape, but we couldn't just walk into the flames of the furnace like sheep to the slaughter.

"Stupid kids thought we were going to kill them for trespassing!"

"You mean . . . you mean . . . you're *not* going to kill us?" I stammered.

"Yeah, right, we're going to burn you in the asphalt furnace," one chuckled. "What an idea," he said to his friend.

This made no sense . . . they weren't going to hurt us. I looked over at Buzz and then Beth. They both still looked scared, but more . . . they looked confused.

"Wasn't that something, the look on their faces when you suggested that!" the second security guard said, starting to laugh again.

"I loved it. Thought the little one was going to wet his pants he looked so scared!"

Me? I wouldn't do that. I was scared but I wasn't going to—

"But why did you say all those things?" Beth asked, her voice cracking

"To scare you, of course," the big one said. "To keep you from ever thinking about coming back here again."

"But . . . but that . . . that was wrong!" Beth sputtered.

"Yeah, well so is trespassing! Besides, you ran and made us chase you down. That really ticked us off! You think we got nothing better to do than chase after a bunch of kids?"

"You're not going to hurt us?" Buzz asked hopefully.

"Of course not."

"And you'll let us go," he continued.

"No way. We're going to have somebody drive you into town to the police station so you can be charged with trespassing and your parents can be contacted."

Oh no, Mom was going to find out. We were still going to die; it just wouldn't be as fast as the asphalt furnace.

"And here comes your driver."

We turned around and my mouth fell open wide.

"Buzz, what are you doing here? And who are your two frie . . ."

Beth and I rushed up and threw our arms around him. It had never felt so good to hold on to somebody.

"You know these three, Samuel?" one of the guards asked him.

"Course I do. The big fella is my neighbour and these two are my grandkids," he cackled.

Grandpa explained things to the guards. They apologized for treating us so badly, but I didn't care about any apology. All I wanted was to get away. I didn't ever remember feeling so many emotions in such a short period of time. As we climbed into the cab of the pick-up truck and I settled in between Grandpa and Beth I felt pure and simple relief. He started up the truck and we drove off, leaving the guards in a cloud of dust.

"Mr. Simmons, what are you doing here?" Buzz asked.

"Can't have a dig at the Money Pit without the island expert now can you?"

"So you work here?" I asked.

"Not really like an employee. More like an investor or partner. All of us are partners. We don't get paid any money but we get part of whatever is discovered. A great deal. The same deal Captain Kidd's men got! A percentage of the booty!"

"But I didn't know you were involved out here," Buzz said. "We've talked about the dig and you've never said a word."

"I couldn't," Grandpa said with a shrug. "Stupid rules of secrecy mean I can't say a thing to anybody. Now it's my turn to ask a question. When did you two get on the island?"

"Today ... this morning on the ferry," Beth answered.

"Didn't take you long to get into trouble. I wasn't expecting you till next week."

"You were expecting us?"

"Sure, don't you always come in July and spend some time with me?"

I looked over at Beth and she looked as unsure of what to say as I did. First off, there was no way he knew we were coming, and second ... it was August.

The truck slowed down. Up ahead was a fence and

a guard house. A guard waved at us and swung the gate out of the way to allow us to leave.

"Um . . . we haven't been here for a while," I finally answered.

"It has been a while. You haven't been here since last July."

"It's been longer than that," I disagreed.

"Don't think so, although I'll agree it does seem longer 'cause I've missed you all so much. Is your mother at the house?"

"That's where she was when we left," Beth answered.

"Good! It'll be wonderful to see my daughter."

"Mr. Simmons, could we make one stop on the way into town?" Buzz asked.

"Can't you hold it till we get home?"

"No, it's not that. I'm okay that way. It's just we rode bikes out here. We left 'em off to the side of the road just up ahead. Could you stop so we could throw the bikes in the back of the truck?"

"I will, but I shouldn't. I should make the three of you walk back out here and get 'em tomorrow."

We stopped and got our bikes. We put them into the back of the truck and continued into town.

All the way as we drove, Grandpa was joking around and being playful. Just like always. It was like no time had passed. Certainly not three years. And the way he talked it was like we hadn't been gone and he hadn't fought with our mother. Maybe he was just being polite, pretending it never happened.

While he acted about the same it was obvious he

didn't look the same. He'd always been thin, but now he looked downright scrawny because he'd lost so much weight. And instead of a neatly trimmed mustache his face was covered by a carpet of grey hair. Finally, there were his clothes. He'd never been what you'd called fashionable, but he'd always been clean. Now his clothes matched the house and were worn and dirty and unkempt.

We turned onto the main street and Grandpa pulled the truck over to the side of the road.

"Okay, all three of you get out," he ordered.

"Get out?" I questioned.

"That's what I said. Get out."

Buzz put his hand on the door handle but hesitated.

"Now! Out!"

Buzz climbed out.

"But Grandpa . . ."

"All of you, out of the truck. Now!" he ordered.

Beth and I slid across the seat and out of the truck. This was just too bizarre. Why was he doing this?

"Okay, now all of you climb back in," he announced.

"You want us to get back in?" I asked in utter confusion.

"That's what I said. Hurry up and get back in or you'll have to walk the rest of the way home."

I climbed back into the truck followed by the other two. Buzz pulled the door closed with a thud.

"There, now I can tell your mother that I picked you all up on Main Street." He turned to us and flashed a smile. "I don't ever like lying, but there's no way I want to tell her about you being out at the Money Pit. Or for that matter, me being out there either. You know how your mother feels about the pit."

I did know. She hated it and thought all the stories about it were stupid.

"We wouldn't have heard the end of that for longer than the time the treasure's been buried in the pit," Grandpa continued.

I laughed out loud. Maybe he didn't remember everything, but he was still the same guy I remembered, and it was so good to see him again.

Chapter Ten

Grandpa turned the truck down the dusty lane that ran behind his house. It was lined by old rickety garages and the brick garages that belonged to the new homes. Some of those new garages were almost as big as Grandpa's whole house. The door to his garage was open and he wheeled the truck right in. We climbed out.

"Could you give me a hand with the bikes?" Buzz asked.

I jumped up on the back bumper and helped him haul down the bikes we'd been riding.

"I better get home," Buzz said and started off on his bike.

As I watched he skidded to a stop and turned around. "Hey, Mr. Simmons!"

Grandpa turned to face him.

"Thanks for picking us up . . . on Main Street," he said with a big smile on his face.

Grandpa chuckled to himself.

"Go on in. I'll catch you in a second," he said. He opened up the hood of the truck and started looking at the engine.

Beth and I filed up the path leading around the side of the house. I took a deep breath of clean air before we entered the house. I walked down the hall and then exhaled noisily. It still smelled, but the difference was enormous. All the windows were open and a fresh, clean breeze ventilated the house. There were a couple of cats perched on the furniture, but the overflowing boxes of kitty litter were nowhere to be seen. Instead there were two very clean boxes tucked into the corners. Papers remained piled in a lot of places but the chesterfield and dining room table were both clear. There was now actually a place we could sit down or eat a meal. The dirty dishes and scraps of food were gone, too.

Mom came out of the kitchen. She was wearing her scrubby clothes and an apron over top of those. She dried her hands on the apron.

"Did you have a good swim?" she asked.

I looked at Beth and then Mom. "We didn't go in the water," Beth said.

"Why not, was it too cold?"

"We were just playing in the sand," I added, being careful not to lie, but equally careful not to say the whole truth.

Beth gave me an approving "way to go kid" look. I

was actually proud of how quickly I came up with that.

I needed to change the subject before Mom asked anything more.

"And we met a new old friend. Do you remember Buzz?"

"Of course. I know the whole family. I used to babysit his older brothers and sisters when I was a teenager." She paused. "What was it you used to call him, Beth?"

Beth blushed slightly. "Buzz off."

I chuckled. "But you should see him now. His hair is longer than Beth's. I guess we're the only ones who still call him Buzz."

Mom gave me a questioning look.

"Well, you know, he used to have a buzz cut and that's how he got his name," I explained.

Mom started laughing out loud.

"What's so funny?" I demanded.

"You don't understand. Buzz *is* his real name," Mom explained.

"They called their son Buzz? Who would call their kid Buzz?" I asked in amazement.

"I remember his mother once told me she called him that because after naming eleven other children all the good names were taken."

"And more important, we also met—"

"What have you done to my place?"

"Grandpa," I said, finishing my sentence.

We all turned to face him. He was standing in the doorway and his expression was one of dismay and confusion and upset all rolled together.

"I just cleaned up a little and—" Mom started to answer.

"Cleaned up! My papers are all out of place!" He screamed and his eyes bulged out of his head.

"They were all over the place," Mom answered calmly. "I just cleared them off the table and a few chairs so we'd have a place to sit and eat."

"Those were the most important papers! Where did you put them? Where are they?"

"I stacked them all in a pile in the corner of your bedroom."

Why was he acting this way? He'd just said how wonderful it was going to be to see Mom, and now this.

He rushed across the room but skidded to a stop at the door to his bedroom

"And why are those windows all open? Close 'em up right away and pull down the blinds!"

"I just wanted to let in a little light and fresh—"

"I don't care what you wanted!" he hollered. "It's my house and you're my daughter so do what you're told!"

Mom's eyebrows arched, her mouth opened and her eyes widened. I held my breath waiting for her response. She closed her mouth and walked over to one of the windows, closing it and pulling down the blinds. She moved to a second window and did the same. Grandpa disappeared into his bedroom but reappeared an instant later.

"My cats! Where are all my cats?"

"They're here . . . most of them . . . a couple might have got out when I was cleaning up and—"

"They're not allowed out! Bad things could happen to them! I've got to find them!" he screamed and ran down the hall.

"Should we go with him?" I asked in confusion.

Mom shook her head. "Stay. Please stay."

"What is wrong with him? What is his problem? He's acting like he's a crazy man or something," Beth said.

Mom walked over and placed her hands on Beth's shoulders. "It's not his fault," she said quietly.

"What do you mean it isn't his fault?" Beth pressed.

"He . . . he doesn't know what he's saying . . . he's confused, and . . ."

I could see that her lower lip was quivering and her eyes looked wet. She turned her back to us. "Maybe you two should go out and help him . . . help him find those cats. I'll get supper started."

Chapter Eleven

I squeezed the toothpaste onto my brush. My image in the mirror above the sink was obscured by so much grime and filth that I wasn't even sure it was my reflection staring back at me. But why should my image be clear? Nothing that was going on here was clear to me.

I wanted to brush my teeth really well. Despite Mom's efforts to clean up after the cats it felt like there was a film of fine kitty litter grit clinging to my teeth. Each time one of the cats scratched away in one of the litter boxes a new wave of particles wafted up into the air.

It turned out that Grandpa had fourteen cats. We followed him around the cottage as he introduced us to each and every one. He did that partially because he wanted us to see the cats, but also to make sure that he retrieved any that had gotten out. In the end there were only two cats that had wandered outside and neither had gone far. They were both just sitting in the front yard in a sunny spot, sleeping. I was amazed by how much he talked about each cat—how long he'd had it, what it was like, and little stories about each one.

I took a sip of water—it tasted like iron—and spat into the sink. The sink was still just as filthy as the mirror.

Grandpa told us more about the cats while we were eating dinner. We knew they were stray cats, but apparently there were some that lived semi-wild on the island. Legend had it that they were the descendants of cats that swam ashore when their ships were sunk off the coast. I could see Mom roll her eyes when Grandpa started talking about sunken ships. I just figured it was far more likely that these particular cats were house cats people put out or left behind when they left at the end of a summer vacation. Grandpa said he'd started with one cat, an old injured one he found half-dead in his garage, and they just kept on coming since then.

Grandpa even told us why he had all the shades drawn during the day. He explained how cats stay awake at night and sleep during the day; the opposite of people. We didn't have a cat, but I knew that. He said that meant that while he was up during the day the cats mostly slept, and then at night, while he was trying to sleep, the cats made such a ruckus that he couldn't sleep well. So he decided to try to change them around. He left lights on all during the night and drew the shades during the day to try to get the cats thinking day was night and night was day. He said so far he was having "mixed" results with his experiment.

Mom had had trouble finding a meal for us. There were lots of cans of things in the cupboards but they were really old; some had swollen and gotten bumps and lumps that pushed right through the metal of the tin. Even I knew that meant there were really bad things going on inside those cans. Things that could make you sick or even kill you if you ate them.

The stuff in the fridge was equally out of date or bad. Beth and I were sent down to the grocery store and brought back a list of things that Mom made up.

Dinner was polite and friendly, which made it a little bit weird. It was as if Grandpa hadn't been yelling and carrying on. It was like the fight he had with Mom when he first got in had never happened, or he didn't *remember* it happening. Just like he didn't remember we'd been gone for three years.

Maybe the strangest part of Grandpa yelling was the way Mom reacted, or I guess didn't react. It wasn't like her to just sit back and take garbage from people. She was more likely to be the one giving it.

I took one more sip of water, rinsed it around my mouth and spat it into the sink. I was going to put down my toothbrush but thought better of it. I put it back inside my plastic travelling case where it would stay safe and clean.

"So you going to show me some of that magic?"

I turned around. Grandpa was standing in the door of the bathroom.

"Sure! Follow me!" I said as I squeezed by him and went into my bedroom. Actually, it was more like a combination storage locker and library, but Mom had managed to cram a cot in. I'd always slept in there since I was old enough not to sleep in a crib in her room.

"Please take a seat," I said to Grandpa, motioning to the cot.

There was a loud creaking sound when he sat and I wasn't sure whether it was the springs of the cot or his bones that made the noise.

"Would you happen to have a five-dollar bill on you?" I asked.

"That seems like a pretty steep admission to the show."

"No, no, you don't understand! The show is free, I just need to borrow it for the trick," I explained.

He reached into his shirt pocket and pulled out a handful of things that he spread out in his other hand. There were a couple of bills, some change and a couple of red and white striped candies all covered in pocket lint. He had a five-dollar bill and two tens. He handed me the five.

"Could you please take that pen and paper off the table beside you. I want you to write down the serial number of your bill."

He picked up the pen and I dictated the number to him. I then took the bill and "put" it into an envelope I pulled out of my other pocket. I licked the glue and sealed the envelope up, placing it in the centre of the cereal bowl I'd emptied for my bedtime snack. I had been hoping to show him a trick and I knew this one would wow him.

"Do you have a match I can use?" I asked.

"No, I don't think I—"

"What about these?" I asked, reaching into the pocket where he'd removed the other objects and pulling out a package of matches.

"Where did those come from?" Grandpa asked in amazement. "I didn't have any matches in there."

I loved that. It was what made magic so magic and why I enjoyed doing it so much.

"I got them from your pocket. Didn't you just see me pull them out?"

What he'd "seen" and what had happened were two different things. I had the package already hidden in my hand when I reached in and "pulled" it out.

I tore one match from the package, turned it over and struck it against the strip to light it. This was a particularly dangerous trick; dangerous because Mom had told me not to do tricks with fire. But it was also one of my best sleight-of-hand tricks and I really wanted to impress my Grandpa.

I picked up the envelope and held the lit match to the corner of it. The paper turned brown and curled and then started to flame.

"What are you doing!" Grandpa exclaimed as he jumped to his feet.

"You've never heard of people having money to burn?" I asked as I dropped the envelope back into the bowl and the whole thing became consumed in fire. Within seconds the fire died and all that remained was a pile of white and grey ash.

"Sit down . . . please."

He hesitated and then sat back down on the cot.

"I don't see how that was magic," Grandpa growled, and for a second I feared he was about to start yelling again.

"It is, really!" I pleaded. "Could you reach in your pocket again."

"I'm not giving you any more money!"

I smiled. "I don't want any more money. Could you please remove the contents of your pocket one more time."

He hesitated and then reluctantly did as he was directed. He pulled out the same objects and looked at them.

"What the heck? Where did this five-dollar bill come from?" he asked. "I only had one and I gave it to you."

"It's yours. The one you gave me."

"What are you talking about? I saw you burn the one I gave you."

"Check the serial numbers."

He turned the bill over and looked at the numbers. His eyes went back and forth from the bill to the paper where he'd written them down. He snorted, shook his head in disbelief and started rechecking them once again. Then he laughed out loud.

"That is some fine trick!" he exclaimed.

I bowed slightly. I felt myself get all warm and happy inside.

"Want to know how it's done?" Beth asked from the doorway.

How long had she been standing there?

"It's not hard. All he does is—"

"Sorry Beth," Grandpa said, cutting her off. "It's been a long time since I did any magic . . . wasn't I the one who showed you your first trick?"

"I was five, or maybe six," I agreed.

"So you're the one to blame for all this," Beth joked.

"That's okay. I'm used to getting blamed for everything. But like I was saying, we magicians know that nobody should ever reveal how a trick is done. Isn't that right, Sam?"

I smirked at Beth, who stuck her tongue out at me. "That is correct. It's bad luck to reveal the magic involved."

"Magic!" Beth snorted. "There's no magic! All he does—"

"Beth!" Grandpa warned her and she stopped.

"Okay, okay," she said.

Actually, Beth was right. It was a very simple trick. All I did was use sleight of hand to palm the bill rather than put it in the envelope. Then when I reached and grabbed the matches I left the five-dollar bill behind.

"Pretty darn amazing trick is what I think," Grandpa cackled. "Much better than the few card tricks I used to do. Anybody want a candy?" he asked, holding out his hand to reveal the two lint-covered candies from his pocket.

"Thanks," said Beth. She hadn't had a close-up look so she didn't know about the lint attached to the mint.

"I've already brushed my teeth," I said as an excuse.

Beth popped it in her mouth and then got a puzzled expression as she quickly discovered the extra layer coating the candy. She reached up with her fingers and plucked out a piece of lint. I tried to stifle a chuckle.

"Are we having a little party in here and nobody invited me?" Mom asked.

"Not a party. A magic show," I said.

She wrinkled her nose and sniffed. No doubt she'd picked up the smell of the smoke. She shot me a dirty look, but didn't say anything . . . although I knew she would later.

"Sammy here is pretty darn amazing," Grandpa said.

"I've used that word, and a few others, to describe him," Mom confirmed. "He's my special guy."

I squirmed a little. I liked her saying nice things about me, but not in front of Beth. I knew what Beth was thinking. I looked over in time to catch Beth as she tried some "sleight of hand" herself. She brought her hand up to her mouth and removed the candy, hoping Grandpa didn't see her do it.

"Maybe it's time for one boy to disappear for the night," Mom said.

"It's still early. Couldn't I read for a while . . . or maybe . . . maybe could I have a story?"

We looked at Grandpa, who was looking at Mom. She nodded her head. "Maybe one story."

Chapter Twelve

Beth crowded under the covers with me in my little cot. It felt good. Just like in the old days, when she and I were close. Grandpa was perched on the edge of the bed. I knew, from all the stories he'd told me before, that it wouldn't be long before he was on his feet. As Mom left the room she'd turned the light off, leaving the room in semi-darkness. The only light was a trickle leaking around the edges of the door from the kitchen. Mom leaving didn't surprise me. She seemed to dislike these stories as much as I loved them.

"So, what would you like to hear a story about?"

"The Money Pit," I said.

"I've told you that story half a dozen times," he said.

"A lot more than that," Beth said. "A lot more . . . but I want to hear it too."

Even in the darkness I could see the thin line of a smile crease his wrinkled face.

"I'll start at the very beginning. Did I ever tell you why Captain Kidd chose to bury his treasure on Oak Island?"

Of course he had. He'd told us a half a dozen different versions over the years and it seemed that each was better than the one before.

"It's been a long time," I finally answered.

"Well, then, it's time you heard the story again. It all takes place over two hundred years ago. Captain Kidd and his crew were sailing the waters south of the island. They were after Spanish ships sailing from the New World with their holds filled with gold. It had been a successful trip. They'd attacked and plundered and sunk five ships. There'd been some damage to Captain Kidd's ship . . . nothing that couldn't be repaired . . . and the loss of more than twenty members of his crew . . . but that was no trouble either. More men dead meant more money for those who lived because the booty was divided among the crew, the officers and the Captain. And, since this was a large haul, the rewards for all would make them rich."

As I'd expected, Grandpa had risen from his seat on the cot and started pacing around the crowded little room. He always got so excited when he was telling a story that it was impossible not to get excited along with him.

"In addition to his crew the Captain had four extra men with him. He'd taken them off one of the ships he'd plundered. They were strangers, natives from far down south in New Spain. When he found them they were below deck, held in irons. Before he put the last of the Spaniards to death he had them tell the story of these men. Apparently they were prisoners who were being brought back to Spain. Usually the Spanish simply killed the natives they captured, but these men were special. They were builders, sort of like olden-day engineers, and they had helped to design and construct the complex pyramids and tunnels and structures that were used by the Mayans. They were being brought back to Spain to build things for the amusement of the royal children."

"I haven't heard this part," I said.

He smiled. "I've only learned about this bit myself the last year. Shall I continue?"

"Of course."

"Captain Kidd wasn't sure if these men had any real value, but he had a feeling they might be of worth to somebody. If nothing else, he figured that the enemy of his enemy might be his friend, and so he spared their lives.

"In that last attack his ship had taken some damage. He thought it best to retire out of the shipping lanes and take refuge farther north. There he could find the hard wood needed to repair the ship. That was how he found himself off the coast of Oak Island, which of course was given its name because of the tall, straight trees that could be found here. And, just as important, he knew there were very few people on the island. And those few people all lived on the south shore, away from where he planned to put in.

"Unfortunately for Captain Kidd, what he didn't know about the island was that the waters off her coast were not a good place to be during the spring months. Storms come up fast and frequently and furiously. And, with his ship already taking on water and tilting under the weight of all the plunder, he was hit full fury with a spring gale."

I thought about how Beth would have handled a storm like that . . . it wouldn't have been a pretty sight.

"It would have been a terrifying feeling, being battered by the waves and rain and winds and knowing that the storm was going to do what no Spanish ship could—send them to the bottom. In desperation the Captain piloted his ship toward land. His only hope was to drive it up onto the shore and run it aground.

"Then, just as all seemed lost, the Captain spied a small gap in the land. It was a cove! He wrestled with the wheel of the ship and somehow aimed the crippled vessel into the cove. Instantly, the ship's tilt lessened. The shores of the cove protected the ship from the full fury of the waves and winds. Providence had shone down upon him. The Captain had all the members of his crew fall to their knees and give thanks to God for their safety."

Grandpa started chuckling until the chuckle changed into a cough and he hacked and hacked until I was sure he was going to cough up a hair ball. Was he okay? Finally it subsided and I felt grateful.

"Funny thing it is. A man like Captain Kidd spends his life stealing and plundering and killing, but still thinks God will take care of him. Doesn't make much sense does it?" he asked.

"Not much," I answered.

"Like not any," Beth added.

"So they put down the anchors and waited out the last of the blow. Starting the next day they began the task of repairing the ship. Some men re-caulked the gaps between the beams, others re-stitched the sails, a few braided new ropes, and the Captain himself led a party onto the island. They needed to replenish the ship's fresh water reserves, gather fresh berries or roots which could fend off scurvy and, most important, fell some oak trees to replace the beams and boards that had been battered and broken."

Once again, Grandpa was striding around the room, talking all excited, making gestures. I couldn't help but feel awed by the way he told a story. It was like a magic trick, but only using words. I wished I could tell a story like that . . . and be so confident talking in front of people.

"The repairs went well. The ship and her stores were soon in good shape. The Captain had even allowed a small party of men to travel by dory to the far side of the island and bring away supplies from the town's general store. Do you know who ran that store?"

We both shook our heads.

"The family name was Turney," he said.

"Turney? Like the people who run the grocery store?" I asked.

"One and the same. The family has been selling dry goods to people on this island for over two hundred years."

Grandpa started hacking again, this time louder and more persistently.

"Hang on a second," he said between coughs and left the room.

The noise of running water rumbled out of the bathroom. This sound was punctuated by a tremendous hacking and spitting sound. Apparently he had coughed up a hair ball. He returned to the room sipping water out of a filthy glass that I had seen sitting on the back of the toilet.

"Are you okay?" I asked.

"Just a little cough. Nothing to worry about," he said. "So with the vessel all 'ship-shape' they set sail. That was when the Captain discovered something he hadn't foreseen. The ship had been able to enter the cove driven by the high waves and strong winds. But those same forces had dumped tons and tons of sand along a bar guarding the entrance. And now the ship, laden with treasure and riding low in the water, was unable to clear the sandbar and make for the open seas. What would you have done if you were the Captain?"

"I don't know . . . maybe unload the treasure . . . and anything else that weighed a lot," Beth said.

"Like the cannons," I added. We both knew the story well enough to give Grandpa the answers he wanted. That was always part of him telling us the story.

"Yeah, the cannons. And then sail the ship over the sandbar and reload it all back on the other side," Beth continued.

Grandpa nodded his head in agreement. "That makes sense, but sense isn't what the Captain wanted. He knew he was being guided by the hand of God. First this cove saved him from going to the bottom, and now it was stopping him from leaving with the treasure. He took both to mean God was giving him a sign: a sign that he should not leave with the treasure, that the treasure must remain here on Oak Island." He paused. "Do you believe in signs?"

"Signs?" I asked.

"Messages from God."

"I'm not sure," I answered uneasily. I felt Beth squirm beside me.

"Back in Captain Kidd's time they took any unusual occurrence as a message from God. Anything they didn't understand was the hand of God."

"They didn't know a lot back then, did they?" Beth commented.

"Funny, they would have thought they were living in the most modern times."

"Modern?" I asked in amazement.

"Modern compared to what went on before that," Grandpa explained.

"But nothing like today," I disagreed. "We've got science and television and computers and the Internet. This is the information age."

"Information," he repeated, slowly shaking his head. "No doubt there's more information . . . more than anybody could ever hope to gather. But you have to remember that information isn't knowledge and knowledge isn't wisdom. There was just as much wisdom two hundred years ago as there is today."

"How do you figure that?" Beth asked. "Those were like primitive times."

"And I guess you two think these are pretty modern times, don't you?" Grandpa asked.

"Not think . . . know," Beth answered.

"Well, if fate smiles on you and you live to a ripe old age, you'll be sitting there talking to *your* grand-kids and they'll be amazed you grew up in such a primitive and old-fashioned time as this."

"Come on," Beth disagreed.

"It seems to me like it's only been a blink of an eye since I was young and the world was so modern. We had automobiles and telephones to the mainland and airplanes! I couldn't imagine anything more that could be invented . . . but lots more was . . . and lots more is still to come."

Beth and I looked at each other with a "what is he talking about" expression on our faces.

"I don't expect you to understand. It'll come in time . . . maybe. Let me get back to the story. Just as the hand of God had brought them to the cove and then trapped them there, it had also given the Captain four skilled men who could help him design the perfect place to hide the treasure." His voice had become lower and lower until the word "treasure" was just a faint hiss hardly audible over the sound of the wind outside the window.

"Over the next four weeks the Captain pressed his men to create the vision planned by the four Mayan engineers. With each layer it became more complex and ingenious and confounding. I suspect that the Captain had no idea how elaborate it would become, and he may not have even agreed to it if he had known. But with each layer he became more and more interested in the creation of the grand design.

"And as for the four Mayans, they probably wished that the digging could go on forever. They knew when it was finally completed their lives would also be at an end. It wouldn't have been wise to allow the designers, the people who knew all the tricks and turns, to go out into the world. Even if they didn't come back themselves, they would be free to whisper secrets to others. And that's why at the very bottom of the pit, even below the treasure itself, rest the remains of those poor, noble men."

"You've found their bodies?" I exclaimed.

"No."

"But then how do you know?" I asked.

"Don't know, just suspect. I'll know soon enough when they get down a little bit farther in the digging. We haven't gotten down as deep as the last dig yet."

"But with all that sand that's been moved, I thought you'd be deeper," Beth said.

"We've moved more sand than ever before, but that's because the hole is mighty wide. But it's getting deeper each day."

"Have you found anything yet?"

"I'm not supposed to . . . shoot, I shouldn't be

keeping secrets from you two. We've found the wood used by the previous digs and—"

"Any treasure?" I interrupted.

"Not yet, but I wouldn't expect to find anything until we get deeper."

"But how can you be so certain there is treasure?" Beth asked.

"The treasure is a certainty. The bones are just my thoughts. The bodies of those four and at least twenty more will be uncovered before we reach bottom."

"Twenty bodies?" I asked. That thought made my skin crawl. "But why so many? You mentioned the four Mayans and I know there were a couple of people killed in previous digs."

"Four men killed trying to dig it up," he said, correcting me. "The other men weren't killed trying to dig up the pit, but rather so they'd never *have* the chance to dig it up."

"I don't understand." Beth said what I was thinking.

"Imagine this. The treasure—gold, diamonds, rubies and other precious jewels—has all been brought off the ship and lowered down into the pit. Sand has been carefully lowered down, and the first few sections have been sealed with oak and putty and stones. Standing at the top of the open pit are the twenty-four members of the crew who've taken part in the digging."

"Why twenty-four?" I questioned. This was another part of the story that was new to me.

"Another educated guess. Researchers think that Captain Kidd had between forty and fifty men on his ship."

"Yeah?"

"Assume twenty were killed plundering the Spanish ships to get the treasure."

"Okay."

"And it takes between four and six men to run a sailed vessel as big as his," Grandpa continued.

"So . . ."

"So if six were on board then he would have had twenty-four men who knew the secrets of the pit."

"But why wouldn't they all know the secrets?" Beth asked.

"Because he needed somebody to help sail his ship away. Do you want to hear this story or not?"

"Of course."

"Then quit interrupting!"

I sealed my lips tightly.

"So maybe these twenty-four know the secrets, not as well as the four Mayans already entombed in the sand, but too well for the Captain's liking. The only men who knew nothing were six sailors who had never left the ship. They were kept in the dark about the exact location of the pit and the secrets and traps it possessed. And the Captain knows one of the oldest of pirate sayings—dead men tell no tales."

I knew where this story was going. It made my stomach tighten.

"So the twenty-four men are standing there, feeling good about the task almost being completed, knowing that their treasure is safe. The Captain reaches into his pocket and pulls out a red handkerchief, and as planned, twelve of the men pull out pistols and shoot the other twelve. Some die instantly while the others must be run through with a sabre. Their dying screams escape into the night air as their blood seeps into the sand."

"But why would they kill their own men?" I demanded, picturing that scene so clearly in my mind.

"Because they're following the Captain's orders. He's approached each of these twelve men and explained the signal and told them the other dozen couldn't be trusted . . . that they were overheard plotting to come back and take the treasure for themselves. They were killed because they were traitors and thieves."

"But weren't they all thieves?" Beth asked.

"Of course they were and there is no honour among thieves."

"And they were killed because Captain Kidd overheard their plans, right?"

"No," Grandpa answered. "He overheard nothing. He just made up the story so twelve more mouths would be silenced. And you know, most of the men who pulled the trigger against men they'd sailed with for years didn't even believe what the Captain had told them. They just thought that twelve less men alive meant a bigger share of the treasure for themselves. Besides, to say no to the Captain might just mean he'd find a man to put a bullet in your head. Better to kill than be killed."

"So the twelve of them finished filling the hole," Beth said.

"Not likely. The Captain would have then given another signal and six of those twelve would have drawn forth a second pistol hidden beneath their cloaks. In an instant, six men would have known that they had been betrayed like they'd betrayed their friends. They were shot dead. Just as suddenly, just as mercilessly, and just as completely. In a matter of less than five minutes the twenty-four men had been reduced to six."

"But it wouldn't have stopped there," I said. "Next three and then two, and then only the Captain."

Grandpa nodded his head. "But only after they'd filled up the hole. At least that's the way I figure it. Now Beth, you go back to your room and go to bed. Sam, you sleep tight . . . and have pleasant dreams."

As Beth climbed out from under the covers I suspected that "pleasant dreams" were about the last thing I was going to have.

Chapter Thirteen

The blinding sunlight streaming in through the window announced it was morning. But judging from how tired I felt it was far too early to get up, especially after getting to bed so late and all the trouble I had finally getting to sleep. About the only thing I'd forgotten about Grandpa's stories was how they kept me awake at night. It wasn't just that they were scary—and most of them were—but that they were so vivid. They'd play over and over again in my head as I lay in bed trying to sleep.

I still felt exhausted. I figured I needed at least another hour or two of sack time. I tried to turn over, away from the bright light, but the covers wouldn't move with me. They must be tucked in too tight, I thought. I reached down to pull them free and my hand was met with movement. I startled and sat bolt upright in bed. There at the bottom of the bed, lining one side, were cats! Six of them all stretched out and intertwined, or curled into balls, were sharing my little cot.

I was too awake now to even try to get back to sleep. I started to pull my legs out from the covers and a couple of the cats woke up. One, a big orange cat, who was missing part of an ear, gave me a mean look. He looked like he could be the offspring of a pirate ship cat. I decided to move slower and more carefully. I slid out of bed and poked around with my feet to find the slippers I'd put just under the bed last night. Finding them I slipped my feet in.

"Yuccckkk!" I yelled as I quickly withdrew my foot from a sopping wet slipper.

The cats reacted to my scream and two scurried away as though they feared for their lives. How could my slipper get soaked? I picked it up and then almost instantly dropped it as both my brain and my nose provided me with an answer: one of the cats had used it as a litter box.

"How disgusting!" I said to the four remaining cats. I had the urge to whack one of them but there was no telling which had done it. Maybe it wasn't even one of the cats that was sleeping with me. Besides, the big orange guy was still sitting there staring me down and I didn't want to get into a fight with him. It was embarrassing enough that my older sister could take me in a fight. I decided it was better to just leave.

I turned and limped a couple of steps before realizing I was still wearing the one good slipper. I took it off, turned around and angrily whipped it at the cats still perched on the edge of my bed. It zipped over the top of big orange and he and the other three scattered like birds. I laughed out loud, but then stopped. I wasn't sure if I'd taught them not to pee on my slippers or got them mad enough to go to the washroom someplace else . . . like in the bed when I was sleeping tonight.

Mom was already sitting at the dining room table. I wasn't surprised to see her there. She always went to bed much later than me, and even Beth, but was always up hours before. She seemed to survive on almost no sleep. I didn't know how she did it. I always got a little cranky when I didn't get enough sleep. I guess that could explain some of her moods, too.

I stood there silently and looked at her. She didn't know I was watching and she always appeared different when she thought she was alone. The look she usually kept locked on her face—determined, serious and in control—vanished. In its place I'd seen her show so much more—soft and gentle, relaxed and thoughtful, and even scared and worried and fragile. That's how she looked now, like the whole world was on her shoulders.

I once tried to explain it to Beth. She'd never seen Mom as I had and didn't know what I was talking about. She'd never seen Mom be anything other than two things—either in total control or out of control and fighting with her. Beth couldn't, or wouldn't, see the parts of Mom I knew were there.

I wanted to go over to Mom and tell her that everything would be okay, but I knew that before I could get halfway across the room she'd put her mask back on. But that wouldn't stop me from putting my arms around her. I knew what was going on behind the facade and I'd do my best to help make things better for her.

"Good morning," I said softly.

"Morning," she answered, her face snapping to attention.

I walked the rest of the way and hugged her hard. She hugged me back.

"I guess Beth is still asleep."

"Will be for hours, I'm sure. At least I know where she is, though."

"What do you mean?" I asked.

"Your Grandpa. I peeked into his room this morning when I got up and he wasn't there."

"I guess he got up early and went out," I suggested. I was pretty sure I knew where he'd gone.

"I hope that's the case. I know he was still awake and puttering around with things when I finally turned in. I'd hate to think he hadn't gone to bed at all."

"Did his bed look slept in?" I asked.

"His bed looks like everything else in this house. I don't think he's made it, or changed the sheets, for a long, long time." She paused. "Did you sleep all right?"

"I guess so. I had a little trouble getting to sleep and then I woke up with cats all around me."

"Me too. I must have shared my bed with at least three of them," she replied.

"But that wasn't the worst part. One of them peed in my slippers."

She shook her head in disgust. "They've destroyed things all over the house. They're more like pigs than cats."

"Why does he have so many, and why doesn't he do something about them?" I asked.

"I guess for the same reason he doesn't do something about a lot of things."

"What do you mean?"

"Bills. He hasn't done anything with his bills for a long time."

"I don't understand," I said.

"Well, here's an example," she said, reaching out for a pile of papers. "Remember I said the phone wasn't working?"

I nodded.

"Well, it isn't out of order, it's been disconnected. He stopped paying his telephone bill about six months ago. He owes almost two hundred dollars and they turned it off."

"But you need to have a telephone to live."

"You need a lot of things to live. Like a house." She paused. "He hasn't paid his property taxes for close to two years." She reached for another stack of papers. "These are past due notices on his property. If he doesn't do something in the next couple of months they can legally evict him and sell the house."

"They can't do that!" I protested.

"Yes they can."

"But, but, we can't let that happen!" I exclaimed.

"We'll certainly try not to, but I don't know where we'll get the money. His back property taxes are close to two thousand dollars. And of course, to top the whole thing off, I just found this," she said, reaching for yet another letter. This one looked very fancy and formal.

"This is a letter from the federal government. Apparently, your Grandpa hasn't paid his income taxes in almost three years and the letter says that legal action may be pursued."

"Legal action? What does that mean?"

"It could mean a lot of things, but people who don't pay their taxes can end up in jail."

"Jail! Grandpa can't go to jail!" I shouted. I felt my whole body get flush with panic.

"Of course not. We're not going to let that happen. That's why we're here."

I knew Mom would take care of things. She always takes care of everything.

"But I'm afraid it's not going to be pleasant and your Grandpa is not going to like it at all."

"I'm still not following what you're saying."

"I guess you wouldn't. I explained a little bit of it to Beth last night after you were in bed, so let me try to explain it to you. You remember the phone call I got that brought us to the island."

"How could I forget."

"It was from Grandpa's doctor. He asked me to come over to the island because he's worried that your Grandpa is no longer competent to care for himself. Do you understand what competent means?"

"Not really," I answered, although I figured it had something to do with his memory and how he was acting.

"Competent means being able to care for yourself . . . to make wise and safe decisions about your life. The doctor thinks that your Grandpa is no longer completely competent and, having seen what's going on, I have to agree."

"So . . . what does that mean?"

"It means somebody has to take control. Somebody has to make decisions, like the way I make decisions for you and Beth."

"And somebody is going to try to make decisions for Grandpa? Like be in charge of him?"

"Not somebody . . . me . . . I'll be in charge."

"But Grandpa isn't going to like that," I said, which was like saying a cat wasn't going to like a bubble bath. "He's always hated being told to do *anything* by *anybody*."

"And that's what's going to make this so much harder."

This was going to make the fights they used to have seem like nothing.

"I wish I knew how he got so far into debt. I know he still has pension money coming in every month, but other than kitty litter costs it just seems to vanish. I can't find any trace of it."

"Maybe he's spending it on the Money Pit."

Mom put down the papers she was holding and

fixed me with a steely gaze. You idiot, I thought to myself, why did you say anything?

"What about the Money Pit?"

"Well . . ." I started to answer, but didn't know what to say.

"Well, what?" she asked sharply.

"Grandpa sort of works there . . . but he's more like an investor or a partner. He doesn't get paid money each week. It's better than that. He gets a share of the treasure when they bring it up."

Mom slammed her hand down against the table and both I and the piles of papers she had been looking through shook and jumped.

"A share of nothing is what people have been getting for the last two hundred years. He's throwing away his life savings, his house, everything for another crack at that wild goose chase! I can't believe it . . . no, that's not right . . . of course I can believe it! Why should now be any different from the rest of his life? Chasing dreams instead of taking care of the things that need to be done. That's just like him!"

Mom never said much about growing up with Grandpa—it was just the two of them because her mother died when she was only ten—but she'd said enough that I knew what she meant. Grandpa had been chasing his dreams all his life, and those dreams often involved treasure and the Money Pit. And when he was devoting his time and money to following those dreams there wasn't time or money for anything else.

"But they're going to get the treasure this time, I'm sure," I protested, protecting Grandpa.

"People have been thinking that for two hundred years!" she scoffed.

"But this time it's different."

"What's different?"

"You should see all the equipment and . . ." I stopped myself, but far too late.

"How have you seen all the equipment?" she demanded.

"Well . . ."

"Did he take you out there?" Mom asked in a tone of voice that said "he better not have."

"Not exactly. We sorta went out on our own and ran into Grandpa there. He drove us back."

"I thought he picked you up on Main Street?"

"Well, technically he did pick us up there, too."

Mom rose from the table quickly and the chair squealed backwards in protest. She looked angry.

"I have to go, I have an appointment," Mom said.

"With who?"

"It doesn't concern you. We'll talk about this when I get home."

I looked at the floor and listened as she started down the hall. I didn't move until I heard the screen door close.

"Nice going, loud mouth."

I turned around to see Beth standing in the dining room doorway.

Chapter Fourteen

Beth moped around the kitchen complaining that there was nothing to eat. There wasn't a lot, but she always complained about breakfast anyway. She was fussy and Mom was always on her about eating. Breakfast was usually their first fight of the day.

I sat at the far end of the table, away from the papers Mom had organized, and pulled out a new magic book I'd bought the day before we'd left. I looked through the book and tried to ignore Beth's complaints.

The first few pages contained the usual introduction, and I skipped over it to the first trick. It showed how to "cut" a rope in two and have it "magically" come back together. It wasn't a bad trick . . . and one I'd been doing for the past two years. I flipped forward. The whole first section contained rope magic and I scanned the pages to see if there was anything I hadn't seen, and done, before. There wasn't. I turned to the index in the back to see if the name of any trick sounded new and different. Nothing jumped out at me. In some ways that was disappointing, but in another way it was almost reassuring. It meant I'd learned so much magic that it was hard to show me something I didn't already know.

"I don't know why you waste your money on those books," Beth said.

I looked up. She was holding a container of yogurt and a spoon.

"I'm not wasting my money. Not the way you waste yours on CDs or make-up," I answered.

"I bet there isn't one trick in that whole book that isn't in one of your other books, is there?"

"Maybe," was the only answer I'd give her the satisfaction of hearing, even if she was right.

"At least when I'm buying music I'm not just buying the same songs over and over."

"I guess not," I agreed, "but what about the make-up?"

"What about the make-up?"

"It's just like magic."

"How do you figure that?"

"You know, you're trying to make your ugly face disappear."

Beth stood up and I wondered if she was going to take a swing at me.

"I wonder if the phone's been fixed yet?" Beth asked.

"It's not broken, it's been disconnected."

"Why would it be disconnected?"

"Grandpa didn't pay his telephone bill."

"But I have to call Brent! I promised him I'd call every day!"

"Brent . . . oh I remember him . . . he's your *friend*." That was the word Beth had used to describe him to Buzz. Did she really like Buzz? And did he like her?

Beth had a look of sheer anger on her face and she took a step toward me. That made two things in a row I shouldn't have said to her.

Just then there came a loud knocking on the front door. "I'll get it. You're safe . . . for now," Beth said. She retreated down the hall.

I looked back down at the book. Of course, Beth was probably right about me wasting money on magic books. Magic was sort of funny; it was amazing when you didn't know how it was done, but once you learned the trick it wasn't nearly as interesting to watch. I always bugged Mom to take me to any magic show that was happening. There were a lot of magicians in the world, but not a lot of good ones. It was hysterical to watch some of the bad ones work. I could almost always see the trick . . . but amazingly most people couldn't because they didn't know where and when to look. That was the secret in trying to figure out a magic trick—always look in the exact opposite place from where they're trying to make you look.

Of course, that wasn't so easy when you were dealing with a master magician. I'd only seen the real pros on television, but they could do some stuff that was way beyond what I knew. A few weeks ago, Mom let me stay up late to watch a David Copperfield special. I even taped it so I could watch it again and again, using slow motion and the pause button. I knew a couple of his tricks, but most of the others were something else. I almost had the feeling this guy wasn't *doing* magic . . . he *was* magic. Watching people like him perform was one of the things that kept me trying out new things.

"How you doing, Houdini?" Buzz said as he followed Beth into the room.

"Pretty good. How about you?"

"Okay. So . . . shall we take another run out to the Money Pit today?"

"Are you crazy?" I asked in amazement. Beth looked just as shocked.

"Naaahhh . . . just fooling with your heads. Between that hound from hell and those guards I'm never going there again. How about hitting the beach? It's still early enough to avoid the tourists."

"I can't go yet. I have to wait for my mother to get back," I said.

"Well . . . I guess you could meet us down there later," Buzz said.

"Us? Who else is going?" I asked.

"I was hoping your sister."

"Beth? You want Beth to come?"

He nodded his head and looked down at the ground. He looked almost embarrassed . . . oh, my goodness . . . he did like Beth. But he was my friend!

"Do you want to come to the beach?" he asked Beth.

"Yeah, sure, that would be—"

"Neither of us can go yet," I interrupted Beth. "Mom won't be too happy if we take off without telling her."

Beth nodded in agreement, although I knew she didn't really want to agree.

"She's probably just gone to see the doctor," I said. That had to be what her "appointment" was all about.

"Isn't she feeling well?" Buzz asked.

"She's okay. I think she wanted to talk to him about our Grandpa." Just as the last word escaped I realized that maybe I shouldn't have said anything. This wasn't the sort of thing you were supposed to tell people; Mom always insisted that family business stay in the family.

"My mom was pretty happy when I told her you guys were on the island," Buzz said. "She's been worried about your grandfather. A lot of people have been worried."

I guess I should have figured that. They were neighbours and old-time islanders and Mom always said that everybody knows everybody else's business in a place as small as Oak Island. That was one of the things Mom really didn't like about the place.

"Mom's going to take care of things," I said.

"She always takes care of things," Beth said, although the way she said it made it sound like that wasn't a good thing.

"Maybe you can meet me down there later on," Buzz said.

"Couldn't you wait? She shouldn't be long," Beth pleaded.

"Well . . . I like to get down there before the crowd comes and—"

"Sam'll show you some magic," Beth said.

"You want me to do some magic?" I asked, dumb-founded.

"Sure. What do you think, Buzz?"

"I guess that would be okay."

"Sit down and I'll go and get us all something to drink," Beth said.

"Sure," Buzz said. He flopped down into a chair as Beth disappeared into the kitchen.

I dug a finger into my ear. Maybe there was so much sand stuck in there I wasn't hearing things right. I didn't know what amazed me more, Beth wanting me to do magic or her volunteering to go and get drinks for us.

"So what are you going to do?" Buzz asked.

"What would you like to see? Cards, coins, rope?"

"Could you pull a rabbit out of a hat?"

"I guess I could. Did you bring a rabbit and a hat with you?" I asked.

"No, of course not!"

"Well, then I can't. How about if I make some-thing disappear instead?"

"That would be good," he agreed. "But I have to warn you, I'm pretty sharp at picking things out."

"Okay, then I better warn *you*. This is very unsta-ble magic. Sometimes I try to make one thing disap-pear and something else vanishes instead."

"Like what?"

"Since you're so sharp you figure it out. Do you have a coin I can use?"

Buzz got up from the table, dug into his pocket and pulled out a quarter. I took the coin from him as he sat back down.

"I'm going to make the coin disappear."

"Hold on," he said, reaching out and grabbing my hand. "Will you make it reappear afterwards or do I get ripped off for my quarter?"

"You'll get your money back," I answered, and he released his grip.

Beth returned to the room carrying a tray with three glasses and a pitcher of lemonade.

"Perfect timing. I need a glass."

I took the glass and turned it over so it covered the coin. Next I reached over and grabbed a piece of newspaper and wrapped it around the glass.

"I will now make the coin vanish!" I said as I tapped the top of the glass with my hand, through the paper. I grabbed the glass, still covered by the paper, and lifted it up.

"Hah! The coin is still there!" Buzz shouted. "Some trick!" he laughed.

"I told you I'm still working on this one," I explained.

Buzz reached for the coin and I reached out to stop him. "Let me give it one more try."

I brought the paper-covered glass back over top of the coin. "The problem was I didn't tap the glass hard enough. Vanish!" I yelled as I slammed my hand down on the paper, smacking it flat to the top of the table.

"What the heck!" Buzz exclaimed. "You smashed the glass!"

"What glass?" I asked as I lifted up the paper. The glass was gone while the coin still sat on the table. "I told you sometimes the wrong thing vanishes."

Buzz felt the table, looking with both his hands and eyes for the missing glass. I scrunched up the paper and tossed it to him. He looked through the paper.

"How did you do that?" Buzz questioned.

That wide-eyed look of amazement in his eyes was the other reason I liked doing magic. As I was about to tell him it was "magic," Beth reached over and plucked the glass off my lap.

"Beth!" I protested.

Buzz laughed. "When did you do that?"

"It wouldn't be magic if I told you."

"Either way, it's still a pretty good trick."

"Not bad," Beth agreed as she poured the lemonade. "It's sort of like all magic tricks."

"What do you mean?" Buzz asked.

"Yeah, what do you mean?"

"They all work the same way," she answered.

"How would you know?" I asked. "You don't even know all my tricks."

"I don't have to know all the tricks to know how they all work. You just have to know the big secret."

"What is it?" Buzz asked.

"Yeah, I'd like to hear this myself," I agreed.

"It's really nothing too tricky. What you try to do with magic is get people to think one thing or look one place, when what's really happening is going on someplace else. Isn't that the trick, Sam?"

"It's a lot more complicated than that. You have to know the specific trick and practise it for hours and have the right presentation and . . ."

"But I'm right, aren't I?"

Maybe she'd been paying more attention than I thought.

"Well . . . yeah . . . sort of. Do you want to see some more tricks or don't you?" I asked.

Chapter Fifteen

"You sure you don't mind me going out for a while?" Mom asked for the third time.

"No, I don't mind," I answered again. "I'll be fine."

"Because it could be a little scary to be alone at night in this house . . ."

"It's not scary."

"It's all right to feel nervous. I remember when I was your age and was left here alone sometimes and how I felt a little afraid."

"I'm not afraid. Would you please just go."

"Sometimes your grandfather wouldn't be home until really late at night and I could hear the floor creaking and—"

"I'll be okay!"

"Fine, I'll go, but I won't go for long," she said.

"Go as long as you want. Don't cut your run short for me."

Mom got up from the table and started to slowly stretch and bend.

"And you know Beth is just down the way," she said.

"I know. If I needed to I could just go down to Buzz's and get her."

"Wouldn't you be more comfortable just going down there while I'm gone?"

"No way!" I protested. "I'm not going to waste my time watching some stupid music video awards."

Besides, I'd gotten the distinct impression that, although Buzz had invited me to come, neither he nor Beth really wanted me along. I couldn't believe he'd rather have her around than me. What about all the fun we used to have?

"When's Grandpa coming home?"

"I don't know," she answered coldly and I instantly regretted my question.

The two of them had been fighting when Beth and I came in from the beach. We heard them before we opened the front door and we stopped and listened for a while. It wasn't just that we were curious about what they were saying but that we really didn't want to be part of it. I couldn't make out a lot of what they were yelling but the little I heard was about the unpaid bills and Grandpa's money going toward the Money Pit. We yelled a loud "hello" when we walked in and they toned it down; actually, they practically stopped talking to each other for the rest of the evening. After supper, Grandpa got into his pick-up truck and drove off. I figured he was heading back out to the Money Pit.

"I could just skip running this one night . . ."

"Go! Just go! I'll be fine!" I practically yelled.

Mom looked taken aback by my outburst, but she closed her mouth and stopped arguing. "I'll see you in a while," she said. She put on the reflective jacket that Beth and I got her for her fortieth birthday and headed for the door.

"Be careful!" I called out.

"I will. Beth is supposed to be home at ten. I should be back a little bit after that. Bye-bye."

Mom had been trying to run once a day for the past few months. She was training to run a ten-kilometre race. I liked her running; she always seemed calmer after she'd been out.

It felt good to be alone. It had been a long day and I was feeling beat. Despite lathering on a lot of sunscreen, I'd had too much of the sun. I'd also had too much of Beth and Buzz.

Beth got on my nerves. That was no big news, but today was different. She had been acting really goofy. She didn't want to dig in the sand or swim or anything. She just sort of laid around on her beach towel and posed like she was in a Sears catalogue. The only thing she did was giggle and laugh at Buzz's stupid jokes and comments.

Buzz hadn't been any better. He'd tossed a football with me for a couple of minutes, but even when he was throwing the ball to me he was looking at her. I wasn't that good at catching a football to begin with and it didn't make it any easier when he kept tossing the ball off in the wrong direction. Other than those few errant throws nobody paid any attention to me at all. It was like I wasn't just unimportant, but completely invisible. I was used to Beth bugging me, not ignoring me, and Buzz was my friend—or at least he used to be my friend.

All they seemed interested in was each other. Talk about *disgusting*. I hope somebody shoots me before I turn thirteen.

I decided to make good use of the time and do something I couldn't do with Mom around—something I'd wanted to do since I first got here. I padded into Grandpa's bedroom. My slippers had been all washed out and now I either kept them on my feet or in the top drawer of my dresser. There was no way I was going to walk around with nothing on my feet because we were continually finding little "treasures" that the cats deposited on the floor.

I turned on the light in his bedroom and pulled open the bottom drawer of his dresser. I smiled. They were there, right where I remembered them being. I knew that Grandpa wouldn't mind me looking; he always showed them off to me and let me look at them anytime I wanted. I would have loved for him to be here to show them to me, but I knew I couldn't ask him with Mom around—there was no point in pouring salt in the wound. Even mentioning the Money Pit got her upset and I didn't like to upset her . . . ever.

Carefully, I pulled out the thick pile of maps. I

knew without counting there would be eleven of them. Eleven treasure maps.

I took the bundle of maps and brought them into the dining room. The table was now completely empty of all papers. The whole house was becoming neater and more organized. Mom was still sorting and cleaning, but now she wasn't telling Grandpa what she was up to and he didn't seem to notice. As long as she left his papers alone he didn't seem to care what she did with the kitchen or bathroom. He even agreed to postpone his experiment to re-program the cats and let us open up the blinds during the day.

I spread the maps out and they filled the table. I took a deep breath. There was a smell to these maps. Sort of musty, dusty and old: it brought back good memories—sitting at Grandpa's side and hearing stories and him showing me the maps and us dreaming about going out to find the treasure together.

Carefully, I looked at each. They were made of different materials, were different sizes: some were old and worn and torn and others were relatively new. A variety of strange symbols and legends dotted some of the maps and while most were written in English, or at least Old English, two were marked with a language I didn't understand; I thought it was maybe Spanish. Despite all the differences, they did have many of the same things in common. Each map showed the outline of Oak Island and the spot just inland from Smith's Cove where the Money Pit was located.

I piled most of the maps together, leaving only

three spread out directly in front of me. These were the three I remembered the most. I recalled so clearly the first time Grandpa had shown them to me. He made me take a vow and swear I'd never reveal the secrets of the map. I was so excited. I couldn't even remember how young I was, but it's one of the first memories I have. It seemed so magical and mysterious, and when he told the story I could picture Captain Kidd huddled over a table in his cabin creating the map. And the map I held in my hand, if not the actual one made by the Captain, was at least a perfect copy of the first map he drew. Boy, it would have been nice to be that young again.

I heard a bustle at the front door. My first thought was that Mom had come back early from her run; I knew how upset she'd be with me for looking at maps of the Money Pit. Then the sound of giggling drifted down the hall and I was relieved. It wasn't Mom, it was Beth and Buzz . . . the names even sounded like a couple . . . Beth and Buzz, sitting in a tree . . . k–i–s–s–i–n . . .

"Hi, Sam. What are you doing?" Buzz asked.

I startled—it was like he'd been reading my thoughts. "Nothing much. Just looking at maps."

Buzz circled around and stood behind me, looking over my shoulder. "Your grandfather has the biggest collection of treasure maps on the whole island."

"You've seen them before?" Beth asked.

"Sure. He had them as part of a display at the library a couple of years ago."

"They made a display of his maps?" I questioned.

"Not just his—lots of people's. There were probably fifty different maps. It was like a promotion to get tourists over to the island. You know, 'discover the treasure of Oak Island,' or something like that."

"I just didn't think there'd be that many maps around," I commented.

"Anybody can make a copy. I know what Oak Island looks like and where the Money Pit is. All I have to do is get some special paper or parchment, look up some squiggly lines or words in a book and voilà, a new old treasure map."

"But Grandpa's are real!" I protested.

"Yeah, sure," Buzz said and Beth giggled in the background.

"They are!"

"Real, I don't know, but I heard a couple of them are worth a lot of money," Buzz said. "They had some historian map guy there at the exhibit and he looked at all the maps. He said three of your grandfather's were very old and one had genuine markings."

"So one of them is really from Captain Kidd?" Beth asked.

"He didn't say that. Nobody could know that. All he knew was that it could be the real thing. He even offered to buy it off your grandfather."

"I'm glad he didn't sell," I said.

"Why?" Buzz asked.

"Because they show where the treasure is buried," I explained.

"Yeah, so what. Everybody already knows where the treasure is buried. He could have sold it for a lot of money and I would have brought him to the pit for free."

"But there's more to it than that."

"Like what?" Buzz asked.

"Well . . . like the writing and the symbols," I said.

"Big deal. He could have taken it down to the drugstore before he sold it and used the photocopy machine. For six cents a copy he could have made enough copies to last a lifetime."

"But . . . it's different," I said, although I couldn't exactly figure out how.

"I don't know why. It isn't like the Money Pit is a big secret or anything. There's been people digging there almost since it first went into the ground two hundred years ago. There are all those books written about it, thousands of maps, and I even heard there's a couple of sites on the Internet. It's got to be the worst-kept secret in the whole world," Buzz continued.

"Or . . ." I started, but didn't know what to say next. I hated to be beaten in an argument.

"Or what?" Beth asked. She had a smug little smile on her face. She was enjoying this.

I looked away from her and down at the maps.

"Or what, Sam?" she asked again.

I had no idea what I was going to say . . . then, like a bolt of lightning, a thought crashed into my brain. I felt like one of those cartoon characters where a little light goes on over top of their heads when they get an idea.

"Or what, Sam?" Beth asked for a third time, her voice much more angry now.

I looked up at her. "Or the location of the money is an incredibly well-kept secret."

"What are you talking about? Even I know where the money is," Beth scoffed.

"No, you don't."

"What are you talking about? Everybody knows the money is in the pit," she said.

"I think it's someplace else," I disagreed.

Beth and Buzz exchanged a look of disbelief . . . or more than disbelief; it was more like annoyance or disgust, especially on Beth's part.

"And you think you know where it's buried?" Beth asked in that same taunting tone.

"I didn't say that."

"Then what are you saying?" Beth asked.

"I'm not saying I know where the money is . . . but I'm certain I know where it isn't."

Chapter Sixteen

"What are you talking about?" Beth demanded.

"The treasure is not in the Money Pit."

"It's not? You figure somebody dug it up already?" Beth asked.

"No, that can't be," Buzz argued. "Anybody who found it would have let people know. It would have been impossible to keep something like that secret."

"Exactly! That's exactly right!" I agreed enthusiastically.

Beth and Buzz exchanged confused looks. "So you *agree* that nobody dug up the treasure?" Beth asked.

"Of course I do. Buzz is right, you can't keep something like finding a treasure a secret."

"So the treasure is still in the Money Pit," she continued.

"No, it can't be," I answered.

"Stop being a little goof, Sam. You can't have it both ways. Why don't you just admit you're wrong?" Beth asked.

"Wrong? I'm not wrong. I may be the only person who *isn't* wrong!"

"Just admit you don't know what you're talking about," Beth continued.

"But I do," I said.

"Sure you do," she said. She turned to Buzz. "See what I have to live with?"

I felt my temper rise. What about what I had to live with?

"Come on, explain it to us, if you can," Beth taunted.

"Why don't you two just go away and watch some more stupid music videos and leave me alone."

"That's his way of saying he doesn't know what he's talking about," she said.

"I do so!"

"Then explain it."

I rose from the table and the chair bumped into Buzz. "I can't explain it."

"That's what I thought," she said smugly.

"But I can show you!" I practically yelled as I ran to my room.

I grabbed my bag and rummaged around in it. I grabbed something and hurried back, dropping the bag.

"Excuse me," I said as I brushed by Buzz and re-took my seat at the table. "I want to show you two a trick."

"A trick! How lame can you get? You think you can use some stupid magic trick to weasel your way out of looking like an idiot?" Beth demanded.

"You don't understand. This is how I'm going to explain it to you."

Beth opened her mouth to argue some more when Buzz put a hand on her shoulder. Her mouth closed and her face softened.

"Let him do it. What can it hurt?" Buzz asked and she nodded in agreement. It wasn't like Beth to meekly agree with anything or anybody so easily . . . except for maybe Brent.

I took the deck of cards out of my pocket and shuffled them vigorously a half dozen times. I put them down on the table in front of me.

"Watch me closely," I said. I pulled my sleeves up so my arms were completely exposed. "You can see there's nothing up my sleeve. Correct?"

"Yeah, so what," Beth answered.

"And you can also see that there is nothing in my hands."

"Or in your head," Beth muttered under her breath.

I turned my hands over slowly and opened the fingers wide to show I was hiding nothing.

"Buzz, I want you to select a card, any card, from anywhere in the deck."

"Can he cut them or shuffle the deck again?" Beth asked. I knew the only interest she had in my trick was to make me look bad by tripping me up if she could.

"He can do anything he wants . . . but I must warn

you both it is important to keep your eyes on me . . .
watch me closely and you may actually figure out the
trick."

"Right, sure," Beth said. "Let *me* shuffle them."

She reached out and shuffled the cards noisily and
then cut them before handing the deck to Buzz. He
selected a card and showed it to Beth.

"Now put it back in the deck."

Buzz did what he was told.

"I want you both to think about the card. Please
concentrate all your psychic energies. I need you to
focus with all your mind."

"Get on with it," Beth growled.

"Or in your case, the little mind you actually
have," I snapped. "And remember, keep watching me
. . . closely."

I stood up and raised my hands high above my
head. I screamed at the top of my lungs and was
pleased when Beth jumped slightly in surprise.

"Are you going crazy?" Beth demanded.

I ignored her. "I'm not getting a clear signal.
Could you two put both your hands on the deck of
cards and squeeze down with all your might and the
card you selected will jump out of the deck!"

Beth and Buzz eyed each other uneasily. Beth
looked like she was going to blush. Buzz put his
hands out, covering the cards, and then Beth did the
same, putting her hands right on top of his. Them
liking each other was nothing short of sick, but it was
just another thing to distract them.

"Now press down. Hard!"

They pushed against the table.

"Concentrate! You have to push down harder!"

I could see the strain in Buzz's face, and the table started to shake ever so slightly.

"There it goes!" I yelled, and they both stopped.

"Where? What are you talking about?" Beth demanded.

"The card, Buzz's card. It flew out of the deck."

"I didn't see any card," Beth stated.

"Neither did I," Buzz agreed.

"Then you're both blind. I saw it as clear as day . . . the eight of clubs."

Buzz's mouth dropped open and even Beth looked astonished.

"That was the card you selected, wasn't it?" I asked.

"Yeah, but . . ." Buzz started to answer.

"But where did it go if it *jumped* out of the deck? Did it fly out of the room?" Beth demanded. She wasn't as easy as Buzz to amaze.

"Of course not. It landed in Buzz's pocket. Front right pocket."

Buzz reached into his pocket and pulled out a playing card. He turned it over to show the eight of clubs.

His eyes widened. "How did you do that?" Buzz asked.

"It's easy," I said. I paused. "Just ask Beth."

Beth's face reflected a combination of surprise, anger and confusion.

"Tell him, Beth. It's like you said, magic is just getting people to think one thing or look one place, when what's really happening is going on someplace else. Isn't that right?"

"Yeah, I guess," she reluctantly admitted.

"But . . . how did you do that trick?" Buzz asked.

"Are you going to explain it to him, or should I, Beth?" I asked and she scowled at me in reply. I'd never done this trick in front of her—not that I hadn't offered before—and both of us knew she had no idea how to do it.

"I guess I'll explain it then. It didn't take any great guess to know you picked the eight of clubs," I said. I turned over the deck and spread the cards out. Every card was the eight of clubs.

Buzz started chuckling and reached out and took the cards in his hands. He looked at them carefully. "Some special deck. But how did you get the card to jump into my pocket?"

"Nothing jumped anywhere."

"Then how did it get in my pocket?"

"I put it there when I brushed by you on the way to my seat."

"You did . . . but why did you pull up your sleeves and get up and yell and tell us we had to watch you?" he asked.

"Because I wanted you to look in the wrong place. That's the magic," I explained. "Now you have to stop thinking of Captain Kidd as being a pirate and start thinking about him as a magician."

"A magician?" Buzz doubted.

"A master of illusion. You have to remember this was a guy who used to carry around flags of different countries so he could get close to the ships he wanted to attack," I said.

"And didn't he do other things to his ship too?" Beth asked.

"Yeah. Sometimes he'd paint insignia and designs on the sails so it would look like a different ship. I heard he even painted the ship once so it would look like a Spanish trading ship."

"That's right!" Beth exclaimed. "And another time he made his ship look like it was abandoned and all the men hid below deck until the crew of the other ship boarded the boat and then they all attacked."

"I didn't know that," Buzz said.

"And I didn't know that *you* knew that," I said to Beth.

"I listened to Grandpa's stories, too, you know."

I shrugged. Of course she had. "And then there was the time Captain Kidd had some of his men dress like women and he put them in a rowboat and when another ship came to rescue them they took over the ship," I added.

Beth started to laugh.

"The money isn't in the Money Pit," Beth said.

"That's what I said."

"Yeah, but you're right."

"I am?"

"Yes, you are."

"He is?" Buzz asked. He seemed even more surprised than I was about Beth agreeing with me.

"Sam is right. It wouldn't make sense for Captain Kidd to do the things he did," Beth answered.

"Like what?" Buzz asked.

"Well for starters, why did he make a map?" Beth answered.

"I guess so he could find the treasure again," Buzz answered.

"He wouldn't need a map to find it. It's like you said, my Grandpa could have sold his map and still found the Money Pit site. It's easy to find," I said.

"Maybe Captain Kidd didn't want to forget," Buzz added.

"No way! Captain Kidd was smart, too smart to need a map. Besides, do you think you'd forget where you buried two million pounds of gold?" I paused for an answer that didn't come. "And why would he put a stone in the shaft telling people to keep digging? If you had gone to all that trouble wouldn't you want them to give up instead of giving them encouragement to keep on going?"

"I forgot about the stone," Buzz said.

The stone was found ninety feet down by one of the expeditions. It was a large, flat stone etched with all sorts of strange circles, crosses, triangles and dots. When those were finally decoded it read, "Forty feet below two million pounds are buried."

"The only reason to do that was to keep them digging in the wrong place. Do you understand?" I asked Buzz.

"I guess."

"It's like you said, Buzz. There can't be any secrets around a treasure. Every member of that crew would know the site of the treasure. That's thirty people who would tell others and the word would spread till almost everybody knew where the treasure was supposed to be buried. And instead he buried it someplace else. Someplace simpler that nobody, or maybe only one or two people who helped him bury it, knew about. Doesn't that make sense?"

"Perfect sense," Beth agreed.

Buzz was rubbing his hand against his face. He looked confused.

"Do you understand?" I asked.

"Sort of. You're saying the Money Pit is like you standing up and screaming. It gets everybody looking in the wrong direction. Well, that stinks," Buzz said as he abruptly got up from the table. "At least before, all they had to do was dig down deep enough and the treasure would be found. Now, who knows? It could be anywhere in the world."

"Not anywhere. It has to be somewhere on the island," I disagreed.

"That doesn't help. It's a big island and it could be anywhere," Buzz said.

"It could be, but I don't think it could be far. It would have been too heavy to drag any great distance."

"That still doesn't help much. What are we going to do, get a shovel and start digging everywhere within a few miles?"

"That's not the way a magician works."

"What do you mean?" Buzz asked.

"You always give the audience a little clue. You show them something and then enjoy it when they don't see it or can't figure out what you did. All we have to do is figure out the clue or where he didn't want us to look," I said.

Beth and Buzz nodded their heads in agreement.

I knew I was right. And I knew that they thought I was right. The money wasn't in the Money Pit. I knew it was buried someplace else. What I didn't know was where that someplace else was. Maybe together the three of us could figure out where it was. And then get it.

Chapter Seventeen

"Hhhhmmmmmm," I said softly to myself.

Was I dreaming or was that the smell of frying bacon? I opened my eyes and inhaled deeply. It was morning and it was definitely bacon. A good way to start the day after a terrible night's sleep. I'd tossed and turned endlessly, punching the pillow and rearranging the covers continually. I'd looked at the time glowing away on the clock on the top of the dresser every few minutes. The last time I'd checked it was almost two in the morning.

Every time sleep came close my mind was overcome with the same thoughts. Was it possible? Had I really figured out the mystery or was I just fooling myself and talking big to impress Buzz and Beth— as a way to finally get a little bit of attention? It didn't seem real. How could an eleven-year-old kid figure out what had tricked so many people for so many years? But . . . it did all make sense, didn't it? Captain Kidd loved to trick people and this would be the greatest trick of all time. I chuckled at the thought of it.

I pulled my legs out of the covers carefully so as not to disturb my bunk-mate, the big orange tabby. Not only did he sleep with me but he'd followed me around the house all last evening. With his missing ear and scowly face he certainly still looked mean, but he was gentle and it felt good to have his warmth against me when I slept. I wondered if Mom might let me take him home when we went. It was funny, I'd never liked cats. They always just did what they wanted—not like dogs who followed orders and tried to please their owners. But there was something about this beaten-up old boy that I liked.

"Come on, Marmalade," I said to the cat. "Maybe I can get us both a drink of milk."

The cat stretched and bounded off the bed after me, rubbing against my legs as I took my slippers out of the top drawer of the dresser and slipped them on.

Last night I'd kept thinking about the maps and how I needed to have another look at them. I wasn't sure what I was looking for, but I knew that was the only possible thing I had to go on. If that one map was for real, or at least a copy of the real thing, then Captain Kidd might have put clues there, clues nobody else would notice. I knew that the Money Pit would be like a bright light blinding people to what was hiding elsewhere on the map.

Just before Mom got back from her run last night, we'd bundled the maps up and put them back in the bottom drawer of Grandpa's dresser. She'd made it clear, especially over the last two days, how she felt about all this treasure stuff and she wouldn't have been happy to see us poring over the maps.

I followed my nose into the kitchen with Marmalade trailing right behind. Mom was at the stove.

"Smells good," I commented.

"Good morning. Did you sleep well?"

"Pretty good."

"It looks like you have a friend there," Mom said, gesturing to the cat rubbing against my legs in tight little circles.

I bent down and gave him a scratch behind his one ear and he lifted up onto his back legs to press harder against my hand.

"Breakfast is almost ready. I'll wake up your sister. Could you go out and get your grandfather?"

"Grandpa's still here?"

"Out by the garage tinkering with his truck."

"I thought he'd be long gone by now," I said.

"He would be. It took the promise of a special breakfast to keep him here. I made all his favourites . . . bacon done to a crisp, strawberry pancakes with real maple syrup and a mushroom omelette."

I felt my mouth start to water. Throw in an Egg McMuffin and those were all my favourite breakfast foods as well.

"I can see why he agreed to stay."

"It'll be good to get a solid meal into him. He looks so thin. I don't know how much weight he's lost, but it has to be at least twenty-five pounds. He's like a walking skeleton."

He did look so old and frail. I started for the door to get him.

"And Sam!" Mom called out.

I stopped and turned around. She motioned for me to come closer, which I did.

"It's important that we take our time with breakfast. I need your grandfather to be here at nine-thirty."

I gave her a questioning look and she continued.

"Dr. Robinson is coming over to the house to see him." She paused. "The doctor needs to examine him, but I couldn't get your grandfather to agree to go to his office. He said he was feeling too good and he had too much to do to waste his time or the doctor's. It's important that the doctor see him."

"Is he sick?" I asked in alarm.

"Not the way you mean," she answered. "It has to do with the things he's doing . . . you know, the way the house is, the cats, not paying his bills, not remembering things."

I nodded. Of course I knew what she meant. "Does Grandpa know he's coming to see him?"

"Not exactly. Dr. Robinson and I went to school together and I mentioned to your grandfather that my friend might be dropping in sometime. Now please go down to the garage and tell him breakfast is ready."

I padded out the back door and along the path to

the garage. I was wondering if I could eat my breakfast out there. I was sure it would be a lot more peaceful than being inside.

Within a dozen steps sand had seeped into my slippers. There was no point in emptying them because they'd refill with sand as quickly as I removed it. Rounding the corner of the garage I spied Grandpa. The hood of the truck was raised and he was sprawled across the engine.

"Morning, Grandpa, breakfast is ready."

"Good, 'cause I'm starving," he said, turning around. "And I'm almost finished here. Could you do me a favour and start up the truck?"

"You want me to start up the truck?" I asked in amazement.

"Unless you want to fiddle with the carburetor while I start it."

"It's just . . . just that I've never started a truck before."

"It's the same as a car."

"I've never started a car either," I admitted reluctantly.

Grandpa snorted. "About time then. Back when I was a boy, and that was long before all these people crowded onto the island, it wasn't unusual for kids eleven and twelve to drive. The keys are in the ignition. Pump the pedal once before you turn the key."

I hesitated for a split second and then circled the truck and climbed in through the open door, closing it behind me. The steering wheel was gigantic, much bigger than the one on Mom's car. I put my foot on the gas pedal—at least I was pretty sure it was the gas, because unlike Mom's car the truck had three pedals instead of two. I pushed it right down to the floor. The keys were dangling from the steering column. I took them in my hand and turned. The engine sprang to life with a roar. I'd started the truck! This was cool. Boy would it be neat to take it out for a little spin. I couldn't wait till I was old enough to drive.

The hood closed with a low thump and I was startled back into reality. Grandpa came over to the driver's side door and leaned in through the window.

"That sounds better. She was running a little fast so I had to adjust the carburetor and set the timing."

"And you know how to do all that?"

"It's not hard. If you'd like I'll show you some time."

"I don't know if I could learn how," I said, shaking my head.

"You're a smart lad, you'd have no trouble. There's a lot of little things to remember but none of them are too complicated by themselves," he explained.

"And you can remember?" I asked. There seemed to be so many things he couldn't remember that were pretty simple.

"Course I can! Been doing it since I was a lad of fourteen or fifteen." He paused and a strange expression came over him, like he was looking at something that wasn't there or was thinking very serious thoughts. I would have given anything to have read his mind. He reached in and turned the engine off.

"Better get inside before that wonderful breakfast gets all cold or all gone."

I had the urge to say something to him . . . ask him about the things that he couldn't remember . . . but I couldn't.

By the time we got up to the house the food was sitting on the table on platters. Beth was seated at the table, although her eyes were closed and it looked like she was still asleep.

"Smells great, doesn't it Grandpa?" I said.

"Looks wonderful," he said as he walked over to the counter and started to wash his hands. "But I have no idea how it smells. Can't smell a darn thing anymore. Lost my sense of smell about two years ago."

That would explain him being able to live with the stench of the cats.

Grandpa and I took seats on opposite sides of Beth, and Mom put heaping servings of breakfast onto our plates.

"This tastes as good as it looks," Grandpa mumbled through a big mouthful of pancakes. "So what are you kids up to today?"

"I don't know . . . maybe go to the beach or hang around," I said. I had a piece of bacon in my hand and slipped it under the table where Marmalade was waiting. He took it delicately from my fingers.

"And call on Buzz," Beth added.

"How about you?" I asked Grandpa.

"The usual. Head out to the pit. Poke around, watch and wait."

"How are things going?" I questioned. I glanced up at Mom and saw from her expression that she didn't like me talking about the pit.

"Stupid rules," Grandpa muttered. "Not supposed to say anything about what's going on. If it was up to me I wouldn't just tell you kids what's happening, I'd show you! I'd bring you along with me each morning."

"That would be great!" I said enthusiastically.

"Would anybody like something else?" Mom asked in a voice that was much, much too loud.

Grandpa shovelled down the last bits on his plate. "No more for me. Everything was great, but I have to get going to the pit," he said, rising from his seat and taking his plate over to the counter.

The clock above the sink showed it was still a quarter after nine.

"Couldn't you stay a little longer?" Mom asked. "Maybe you could have a second cup of coffee, or a muffin? I'll put some in the oven, it won't take long . . ."

"Thanks, but no thanks, I have to get going. I better hit the can before I go," he said as he disappeared into the bathroom.

"He's got to stay," Mom said in a hushed voice. "The doctor's doing me a big favour coming out here this morning. We have to keep him here a little longer." Her mask had slipped slightly and she sounded desperate. She needed my help.

The toilet flushed and he came back into the room, tucking his shirt back into his pants.

"Grandpa. Could you show me your maps?" I asked.

He finished tucking in his shirt and looked up. "The Oak Island maps?"

"Please."

"You always did like those maps. They're in the bottom drawer of my dresser. Help yourself."

"Couldn't you show me?"

"Show you? You've seen them before, a dozen times, and I've got to get going. Don't want them to think I'm not coming."

"Please . . . it would be . . . special. Like when I was a kid."

He shook his head and a smile pushed its way through the stubble and wrinkles on his face.

"For a few minutes. Go and get them."

I hurried off and quickly returned with the maps. I wanted to spread them out on the table again but couldn't because of all the breakfast things. Beth continued to eat, in slow motion, with her eyes still closed. It looked like she was sleep eating.

"Bring them here," Grandpa ordered and I handed them over.

He sat down on the couch and I took a seat right beside him. He started to spread them out on the coffee table.

"Buzz was telling us about your maps being on display at the library last summer," I said.

"Yep, mine and a lot of other people's."

"And he said some expert guy said you had one of the best."

"Not one of the best . . . the best. He told me it was worth a lot of money," he said, picking out the smallest map and showing it off. "The age of it, the markings, even the type of ink all match Captain Kidd's ship's log."

"Where did you get that one from?" I asked.

"That's a long story. One I've not the time to tell this morning. It's enough to say it found its way all the way up from the West Indies. A little money and a lot of rum changed hands that night," he said with a chuckle.

"It must be worth a lot of money!"

"It's worth more than money," he answered.

I was just going to ask him what he meant when there was a knock on the door.

"I'll get it," Mom sang out.

I looked up at the time. It was a few minutes before nine-thirty. Mom returned with a man who must have been the doctor.

"Tommy! How are you doing?" Grandpa asked.

"I'm doing fine, Mr. Simmons. And yourself?"

"Couldn't be better. Working away at the Money Pit for starters and . . . oops, I'm not supposed to be talking about that."

"I'm sure it's okay," Dr. Robinson said.

"And of course having my daughter and grandchildren here is even better. These two are Beth and Samuel. He's named after his old grandpa. Say hello to Tommy Robinson . . . Dr. Robinson."

"Good to see you again, kids," he said and we both half-nodded, half-waved.

"And of course there's my daughter, Rebecca, I don't know if you've met her before," Grandpa said.

"Um . . . we went to school together," Doctor Robinson said.

"I told you that yesterday," Mom said softly.

"You did? Oh yeah, that's right. Sometimes the memory doesn't work so well. I've had so much on my mind these days. What brings you around here this morning?"

"I've come to see you."

"Me?"

The doctor nodded. "You didn't come for your appointment last week . . . the one you promised to keep after not showing up for the last two."

"Must have slipped my mind. Been so busy up at the pit. Sometimes I'm putting in sixteen- or eighteen-hour days. I'm probably too old to be working that hard but I love it just the same. Besides, it seems like a waste of both our time. I feel fine!" Grandpa protested.

"Glad to hear you're feeling good, but I was starting to take it personally, you not showing up," the doctor laughed. "Now that I'm here, how about if we talk for a while."

"Always willing to talk . . . except of course I can't say a word about the pit."

"That's okay, I was actually hoping to talk about you."

"What about me?"

"Nothing serious. Could I ask you a few questions?"

Grandpa passed the little map over to me and stood up. "Sorry, I don't have the time for this. They're expecting me down at the pit."

"It'll just take a few minutes," Doctor Robinson insisted. "And it is the law."

Grandpa stopped in his tracks. "The law? What are you talking about?"

"Mr. Simmons, I have some concerns and I need to talk to you."

"You are making no sense whatsoever, Tommy."

"It's just that people are concerned . . . your daughter is concerned . . . about your memory . . . about how you're running your affairs and taking care of yourself."

"You think I've gone batty, don't you?" he demanded loudly. "Both of you think that, don't you?" he said, turning to Mom.

"Nobody said anything about being 'batty,' Mr. Simmons, it's just that my concerns as your doctor—"

"Well, who said anything about you being my doctor? Your father's been taking care of my health for the past forty-odd years and he's the only one I'm listening to. If he wants to talk then I'll talk! If not, I don't want you wasting my time! Matter of fact, when I'm through with work tonight I'm going to march right into your father's office and have a talk with him. And knowing your father the way I do, I know he'll be none too happy with you! Now, I got to get going!"

Grandpa marched across the room, grabbed his jacket and cap off the rack and was gone. All at once everybody took a deep breath, like they'd been holding it, waiting for him to leave. Mom looked like she was on the verge of tears. The mask slid farther down.

"Is Grandpa good friends with your dad?" I asked Dr. Robinson, giving Mom a second to recover.

"They grew up together here on the island. Your grandfather was best man at my parents' wedding."

"Maybe he'll listen to your father," I said hopefully.

"You don't understand, Sam. My father is dead. He passed on about five years ago."

"But . . . but . . . doesn't Grandpa know?"

The doctor shook his head slowly. "He spoke at the funeral. He was even one of the pallbearers." He turned to Mom. "This is very hard . . . and very sad . . . but I don't think we have any choice. I have enough information. I'll make up the papers."

Chapter Eighteen

Dr. Robinson and Mom excused themselves and went to the kitchen. They had things to talk about that they didn't want Beth and me to hear. Beth obliged by going back to bed. How could she just go back to sleep like that? How could she just pull the covers over her head and pretend nothing happened? I stood close to the kitchen door trying to hear snippets of what they were saying. I could only pick out a few words of the conversation, but the tone was clear: serious and hushed. I jumped back as they came back in through the door. I felt guilty.

"I'm sorry . . . really sorry," Dr. Robinson said.

"For what . . . what's going to happen?" I asked.

The doctor looked toward my mother. She nodded her head.

"Please sit down, Sam."

I took a seat at the kitchen table again. The doctor took a chair and moved it in close to me. My mother took another chair and positioned it just off to the side.

"Sam, have you ever heard of Alzheimer's disease?"

I shook my head. Now that I was going to find out what was happening all I could think about was how I wanted to jump up and run out of the room.

"It's a condition that mainly affects the elderly."

"Grandpa isn't that old . . ." What was I saying? Of course he was old.

"It starts with small things. Not being able to remember names or where they've put things."

"That happens to me sometimes," I protested.

"It happens to us all," Dr. Robinson said. "But it's more than just sometimes. I know it's hard Sam, but you know things aren't right."

I couldn't argue with that. "Does it get worse . . . will he have more problems than he has now?"

"It's different with different people. With some it's a very fast-moving disease. Things can deteriorate very quickly, but with others it can be very slow."

"Can anything fix it?" I asked. "You know, an operation or medication?"

"There is a drug."

"Then we have to get it for him!" I exclaimed.

"It doesn't stop things . . . just slows down the course of the illness." He shrugged. "I'd be in a much better position to make a prediction if I could sit him down long enough to do a full assessment."

"Maybe we could get him to your office," I said.

"There's not a chance," my mother said. "I've been around him my whole life and when he's into one of these wild goose chases of his—these treasure hunts—he doesn't have time for anything!" She jumped up from her seat and walked across the room, turning away from us. "No time to eat, sleep . . . or for his family."

Before Beth and I came along the only family Grandpa had was Mom. I got up from my chair and went to her side. "Mom, are you okay?"

"I'm fine," she said. I could hear the strain in her voice and could tell she was fighting back the tears.

What could I say, how could I make this better?

"Rebecca," Dr. Robinson said. "So your father hasn't been sleeping or eating very well?"

"Terrible, just terrible, probably for weeks or even months while this pit business has been going on . . . why?"

"It may mean nothing. It does make it more difficult to make an accurate assessment. Regardless, we have to go through with the next steps. Why don't you come down to my office now."

"Fine, I'll get my bag," Mom said as she walked out of the room.

Dr. Robinson got up and placed his hands on my shoulders. "I'm terribly sorry, Samuel, very sorry."

"Thanks," I said. I knew he wasn't nearly as sorry as I was.

I sat at the coffee table alone, looking at the map. The one, special map. Last night all I could think about was having another chance to see the tattered old map that I was now holding in my hand. Now, I was almost afraid to look. I knew the only chance I had of solving this mystery, and proving my theory, was somewhere on this map. And if it wasn't there it wasn't anywhere. Slowly, I turned it over.

It was on a piece of thick parchment that had probably been white at one time, but was now yellow with age and handling. The edges were ripped in a few places and all the corners were rounded. I rubbed the map between my fingers. It *felt* ancient.

Unlike some of the larger maps, which were written in different shades of ink, it was drawn only in black ink. The outline of the island was visible although in places it had smudged and faded. Just in from Smith's Cove was the clear site of the Money Pit. It was marked with an X and an illustration of a few "pieces of eight." At the sides of the map were a variety of symbols and words: a legend showing distances at the bottom left corner, a compass in the top right, a chart showing tide times, and depth readings all around the cove. In the waters all around the island there were pictures of fish and mermaids and octopi and whales.

I was confident that if there was a clue it had to be right here in front of my eyes on this map. I looked hard, trying to figure out what could signify a clue. There was virtually nothing on the island itself except for the X by the Money Pit. I was thinking that maybe there was a dot or something that would indicate another possible site. If there ever was something there, it was gone now. Maybe it had worn off with all the handling.

Next, I turned to the outline of the island. Perhaps Captain Kidd had deliberately changed the shape and that would indicate where the treasure really was. I compared the outline to the one on the two other "good" maps. If there was a difference it was too small for my eyes to see.

What about the compass? Maybe it was "pointing" to the treasure. It was in the top right corner and none of the points, north, south, east or west, aimed at the island. Nothing there.

How about the depth readings? Maybe they were false and the numbers gave co-ordinates for the treasure or . . . but who was I kidding? How could I find out what the depth readings really were, and wouldn't they change over the years anyway? And what did any of it matter anyway? What about my Grandpa? What was going to happen to him? How was this all going to end?

My eyes got blurry and I rubbed them with my hands. A wave of tiredness overwhelmed me. Of course I hadn't slept well again last night, which made two in a row. Maybe that was why I couldn't figure this out, because I was just too tired. A few minutes sleep might make a difference. Maybe I could just put my head down and close my eyes. I rested my head on the map on the coffee table. Just a few minutes . . .

"Wake up!"

"What . . . what?" I answered as a hand shook me and I sat up, half awake.

"You've drooled all over it," Beth said, pointing down to the map.

I rubbed the corner of my mouth with the back of my hand and looked down at the map. There was a small wet mark on the island. I felt embarrassed.

Beth reached down and grabbed the map. "Is this the really valuable one?"

I nodded.

"And you decided to use it as a pillow."

"I was tired . . . I didn't think I'd fall asleep on it. I was just trying to figure out the clues," I explained defensively.

"Clues? Hah! Do you really think you can find an answer that everybody else has missed for the past two hundred years?"

"I thought you believed my theory."

"I believe the money isn't in the pit. I don't believe that you can figure out where it really is."

"Maybe I can," I replied meekly.

"Yeah, right," she scoffed. "Have you found anything yet?"

"Not yet . . . but I'm still looking."

"Is that how you look, with your eyes closed? You're just lucky your drool didn't smear anything."

I stood up and looked at the map over her shoulder. The small stain of drool was located square in the top part of the island, well away from the Money Pit, and it didn't touch any ink. Thank goodness. Once it dried, even if it did stain, it would just blend in with all the other stains on the yellowing parchment.

"It would have been bad if you ruined the fish or the other drawings," Beth noted.

She was right. The illustrations were all very detailed and intricate. Somebody had gone to a lot of trouble to make them look realistic. Whoever had drawn them was a real artist . . . strange . . . the whole map was simple and plain—nothing there but information and facts, things you'd need to navigate the waters and then dig up the treasure. But the drawings of the sea life were so elaborate. It didn't make sense. Why would somebody go to so much trouble to draw these pictures?

"Beth, let me have the map back."

She turned away from me, shielding the map with her body.

"What are you doing?" I demanded.

"Keeping the map safe from your drool."

"Beth, quit fooling around!"

"Who's fooling around? We can't have you messing up this map anymore," she taunted as she held it in one hand high above her.

"Beth, I have to see it!"

"You see with your eyes, not with your hands."

"I want to see it. Now!" I ordered.

Beth looked surprised. "Sure."

I took it from her and walked over to the window where there was better light. Somewhere in those illustrations was the key to where the treasure was buried.

"What's gotten into you?" Beth asked.

I looked up. "An idea has gotten into me."

She stopped. "An idea? Do you know where the treasure's buried?"

"Not exactly," I admitted.

"Then what are you talking about?"

"I don't know where the treasure is, right this second, but I'm pretty sure I know how to find out. Come here and have a look at the map. Look at the pictures," I said.

Beth leaned over.

"You see how they're different from the rest of the map? It's like one person made the map, you know, drew the island and all the legends and words, and somebody else drew the pictures."

"Yeah, so what does that mean?"

"In magic nothing is ever done for no reason. Everything has a reason, and there has to be a reason for these illustrations."

"Maybe they're just there because they're, you know, pretty," Beth said.

"That's not it. Somewhere in these pictures is the clue we're looking for."

Beth took the map back from me. She looked at it carefully and then turned it upside down.

"Everything else is right-side up, except for three of the whales," Beth said, pointing to three of the illustrations; one was upside down at the top of the map while the other two were sideways.

"And it's not just that they're different that way. Look at how they're drawn," I said.

"You're right. The rest of the illustrations look like a real artist drew them but those three look like they were made by whoever made the rest of the map," Beth added.

There was a knock at the door.

"I'll get it," Beth volunteered, and trotted off down the hall.

I knew she was hoping it was Buzz. I didn't care if it was the Queen of England. About the only person I wanted to talk to was Captain Kidd. He could have answered all our questions, although I suspect if we had ever met him in real life he would have either laughed at our efforts or run us through with a cutlass as punctuation at the end of our first question. After all, he was a pirate. A real, true-to-life pirate. I bet nobody ever called him a "mama's boy"—or at least lived to talk about it.

I looked at one whale, spun the map around, looked at the second, and then spun it again to see the third. They were all identical: crude, badly drawn whales with five sprays of water shooting out of each blow-hole. I turned the map back around to look at all three. Four of the sprays on each were short and the water just curved back toward the whale, but on each the fifth column, the centre fountain, was tall and straight . . . like an arrow . . . pointing toward the island.

"Beth says you're still trying to figure out the secret," Buzz said as he entered the room followed by Beth.

"No I'm not," I answered.

"You aren't?" Beth asked. "You mean you've given up already?"

"No . . . I'm not trying to figure it out . . . I have."

Chapter Nineteen

"Beth, get me a pencil and a ruler."

"What do I look like, your servant or—"

"Just do it!" I ordered. I think my tone surprised her. I kept my eyes on the map, like I didn't want to look away in case what I saw vanished like a mirage.

"Now!"

She hesitated for an instant, muttered something I couldn't hear, and then went into the kitchen. Buzz came over and sat down beside me. He stared at the map as well. I could hear drawers opening and closing in the kitchen as Beth searched.

"Will this do?" Beth asked as she reappeared. She was holding a wooden paint stick and a pencil.

"Yeah, as long as it has a straight edge," I answered and she handed them to me.

I placed the edge of the stick along the straight

spray of one of the whales. Then with the pencil I started to extend the line onto the island.

"Are you crazy?" Beth demanded, snatching the pencil away from me.

I grabbed the pencil back. "No, I'm not crazy!"

I put the lead of the pencil against the paint stick and continued the line until it dissected the island.

"Grandpa's going to kill you!" Beth said.

I spun the map around and placed the stick against the straight spray of the second whale. I began to extend that line with the pencil.

"Are you sure you should be doing this?" Buzz asked uneasily.

I didn't answer. I extended the line until it reached the first line I'd drawn. I spun the map a third time.

"Sam, you can't just scribble all over this map!" Beth said.

"It's worth a lot of money . . . or at least it *was* worth a lot of money before you drew all over it," Buzz said.

I hoped I knew what I was doing. I took a deep breath. "It's a treasure map and I'm finding the treasure."

I took the straight edge and laid it down against the spray from the third whale. Carefully, I lined it up and pressed the pencil against the edge. Slowly, I lengthened the line until it reached the island and then . . . stopped. It almost felt like my heart had stopped beating, too, I had such a rush of excitement. The third line had hit exactly where the other two lines connected— there was a spot where all three lines joined together.

It was a few miles north of the Money Pit and about the same distance from the water.

"That is where the treasure is," I said, pressing my finger against the spot.

"There?" Beth asked in disbelief.

"Right there," I said, tapping my finger repeatedly on the spot to make the point. "It isn't an X but that's where the treasure is buried."

"Just because some stupid lines join doesn't mean that's where the treasure is," Beth protested.

"It does. It's buried right there," I argued.

"The only thing that's going to be buried is you when Mom and Grandpa find out what you did to the map!"

"Wait," Buzz said softly. "Just hold on a minute." He bent low over the map and his face got all scrunched up like he was thinking or was constipated.

"Do you know where this is?" he asked, placing a finger on the connected lines.

"Where the treasure is buried," I answered confidently.

"This is right about where Humpback Hill is," Buzz said, answering his own question.

"Humpback Hill?" Beth and I asked in unison.

"Yeah. I don't think that's its real name . . . I don't think it has a name. That's what the people on the island call it. It's a rock, a big rock, and the way it's shaped it looks like the back of a whale breaching the water."

We all looked at each other.

"How big is it?" I asked.

"Pretty big. From the top you can see almost the whole island. Lots of people use it to practise rock climbing," Buzz said.

"Rock climbing?" Beth questioned.

"You know. They have all sorts of equipment and they climb up the side of things. I've been out to watch them. It's pretty high."

We all fell into an uneasy silence and stared down at the map. I looked up at Beth, and then at Buzz. Both stood there wide-eyed and open-mouthed. A smile creased Beth's face and Buzz chuckled. It was a nervous little laugh. Buzz looked like he wanted to say something, and gestured with his hand, trying to make a motion to support words that weren't coming out of his mouth. My mouth felt as dry as cotton and I cleared my throat and swallowed hard.

"Sam . . . do you really think . . ." Beth finally started to say.

I nodded my head.

"That the treasure is buried there," Beth said, touching the spot on the map.

I was impressed that she'd been able to produce words. I nodded again.

"Then . . . what should we do now?" she asked.

Buzz giggled. "Treasure hunting. We should go treasure hunting."

Within twenty minutes we were on the road to Humpback Hill. Half that time had been wasted by Beth and I arguing about whether we should leave a note saying where we were going and if we should take along the map. We finally agreed: the map came with us, and a note was left but said we were just "going out for a ride" with Buzz and that we'd be back by three o'clock.

We rode along in single file, with Buzz leading the way. I was in the middle and Beth took up the rear. It was still pretty early and the traffic wasn't that bad once we left town. Buzz suddenly dropped back until he was beside me.

"I was wondering. How could Captain Kidd get his treasure off the ship and bury it someplace else without his crew knowing it?" Buzz asked.

"I was thinking about that too, and I think I have some of the answer."

"An answer to what?" Beth asked as she pushed her bike harder until she was on my other side.

"An answer to how Captain Kidd could get his treasure off the ship without anybody knowing where he really buried it," I explained.

"Well?" Buzz asked.

"If you were the Captain of a ship filled with pirates, men who were liars and cheats and murderers, where would you keep your treasure?" I asked.

"In my cabin, maybe even under my bed," Beth answered. "Or at least someplace where I could keep an eye on it."

"That makes sense," Buzz agreed. "I wouldn't want to let it out of my sight."

"And how long do you think the ship was in Smith's Cove while they were digging the Money Pit?" I asked.

"I don't know . . . a long time . . . maybe a month," Buzz replied.

"Maybe longer. And during that time do you think the Captain would be free to come and go as he liked?" I continued.

"Of course. He was the Captain, and I don't think he would have liked anybody questioning his authority," Buzz said.

"That's right. All of your answers are what I think too, so I figure he could have done it little by little."

"What do you mean?" Beth asked.

"I think he took his time. He probably left the ship two or even three times every day. If they were there for say, three months, that means he left the ship maybe four hundred times. What if every time he came to shore he brought with him some of the treasure . . . not a lot, but maybe ten or fifteen pounds of gold or jewellery hidden away in his socks or his boots or the seams of his coat?"

"Yeah," Beth said.

"Then he could have moved a whole lot of treasure off the ship without anybody knowing it," Buzz added.

"And what if he had one, or even two people that he trusted. The three of them could remove even more treasure. Every time one of them left the ship he visited the Money Pit, where everybody was working hard—"

"And instead of going straight back to the ship," Buzz said, "they take a little side trip to a deserted spot a few miles away where there's another pit that's been somehow covered over so nobody can see it."

"Exactly!" I confirmed. "That makes perfect sense."

"And they take the bit of the treasure that they've hidden and toss it in the hole and then they stuff their pockets with rocks to bring back to the ship," Buzz continued.

"Rocks? Why would they bring rocks back?" Beth asked.

Buzz smiled. "Do you know, Sam?"

"I . . . I don't know," I said, shaking my head.

"To put back in the treasure chests," Buzz explained.

"Of course! That would be perfect!" There was a lot more to Buzz than I gave him credit for.

"I still don't understand," Beth admitted.

"So that when they finally carried the treasure chests to the Money Pit nobody would be tipped off because they'd still be heavy, like they were loaded with treasure," Buzz explained.

"And maybe some of them still held some treasure . . . a thin layer of gold at the top so the Captain could open up the chests and everybody would see the treasure was still there," I added. "While most of the treasure was really buried in a shallow hole close at hand."

"Why shallow and why close?" Buzz asked.

I liked that I still had some answers nobody else had.

"It had to be close because the Captain would have had to make so many trips without anybody noticing he was gone, and it would have been shallow because he wouldn't have had time to dig deep. Besides, it didn't need to be deep," I explained.

"Because . . ." Buzz asked.

"Because everybody's going to be wasting their time digging elsewhere. Nobody knew where the treasure was really buried so it didn't have to be very far below the surface. Just deep enough so nobody would stumble on it for a year or so."

"A year or so . . . wait a minute," Buzz began. "Even if you're right about everything and the treasure was buried at Humpback Hill, what makes you think it's still there?"

"If somebody had discovered it we would have heard all about it, like you said before," I reasoned.

"If *somebody* had discovered it, but what about Captain Kidd? Why didn't he come back and get it?" Buzz asked. "Wasn't that his plan?"

"That was his plan. What he didn't plan was getting caught and tried and hanged."

"Hanged? Like killed?" Buzz asked, putting one hand up to his neck.

"Like dead. Captain Kidd and his crew were captured less than a year after leaving Oak Island. If that treasure was ever there . . . it still is."

Chapter Twenty

Buzz had us stash our bikes by the road a few miles from Humpback Hill. It was the same road that we took to get to the Money Pit and I felt uneasy following the same route. Leaving the bikes, we started to walk across the sand and soil, heading for a low rise that Buzz pointed out in the distance. He said it was Humpback Hill. It didn't look much like a whale, and from this distance hardly looked like a hill. That was good. The smaller the better.

We followed along a small, badly worn trail that wound around clumps of trees, a couple of small hills and some rocky outcrops. It was obvious that while some people came out this way, they weren't many.

As we got closer it also became obvious that Humpback Hill was big, much bigger than it looked from the road. This was not good news. The bigger the hill, the larger the area where the treasure could be buried. The map had got us this far but hadn't told us exactly where the treasure was buried. I knew that we couldn't just start digging because it would take us forever to dig holes all over the hill. I just hoped something would jump out at me and give me the last little piece of the puzzle.

"Can we stop and have a drink?" Beth asked.

Buzz nodded and we all sat down on some rocks. We took off our backpacks and pulled out our water bottles.

"Here, I brought an extra water bottle for you," Beth said, handing one to Buzz.

I noticed their hands touched when he took the bottle and they both started blushing. Gag me with a spoon . . . how could these two be so goofy?

I brought the bottle up to my mouth and took a long sip of water. It felt cool and refreshing.

"This is a lot farther than I thought it would be," I commented.

"Far from the road, but not that far from the water. We're coming at it from one side and the Money Pit and ocean are in slightly different directions, but on the other side. You'll be able to see both when we get to the top of the hill," Buzz explained.

"Sounds like it has a good view," Beth said.

"It's the highest spot on the whole island. From up on the top we'll be able to see the town, the outline of most of the island, the work going on at the Money Pit, and even the ferry if it's coming or going."

"It sounds perfect," I stated.

"I don't know about perfect, but it is nice," Buzz replied.

"No, you don't understand. It's perfect if you want to hide something because you can see if anybody's coming in any direction." I got up and put my pack back on. "Let's get going."

We started moving again. The trail became rougher and more difficult to follow. Instead of sand, we were travelling through stands of small trees or over sections of bare rock. Despite the difficult terrain, I found myself moving faster and Beth and Buzz called after me a few times to slow down. I wasn't interested in slowing down. If it was up to me we would have run the rest of the way.

Besides, I wanted to be by myself, and it wasn't just to get away from Beth and Buzz giggling and making cute little comments to each other. I was nervous. What if I was wrong? What if there was nothing up here and I'd dragged all three of us on nothing more than a wild goose chase? But how could I be wrong? Didn't it all make perfect sense? I laughed to myself. It was stupid to think that in a few minutes I'd solved something that had fooled thousands of people for two hundred years . . . but then again maybe that's just the way it worked. Millions of people could watch a magician on TV and be fooled. Only another magician would know the truth.

It felt like I was on a roller coaster, with my emotions and confidence going up and down and up and down.

I looked back. Beth and Buzz were no place to be

seen. I'd almost started back down the path when they appeared around a bend. I stopped and waited until they got closer and then started off again. It may have been a bright, sunny morning but somehow it felt more than a little spooky to be out there when I was alone for those few seconds. It was reassuring to have them in sight. Thank goodness it wasn't night time. It would have been terrifying to be here in the dark.

I rounded a grove of trees and found myself standing right in front of the hill. It was a steep, almost straight-up face of rock. It was marked with vertical veins that ran the whole length of the face. I could see how rock climbers would enjoy scaling the side. What I couldn't see was any possible way we could get up there without special equipment. And, even more troubling, that magical place where the treasure could be buried hadn't materialized yet. I heard a sound and looked around. Buzz and Beth were just a few steps behind.

"I didn't think it would be this steep or high," Beth commented.

"It's both of those . . . at least from this angle," Buzz replied.

"It's lower someplace else?" I asked.

"It's lower everyplace else. This is the whale's head. We can walk along either side and it gets lower and lower until it disappears into the ground completely. Come on, I'll show you."

We followed behind Buzz. At first I didn't see any difference. We walked along with the sheer wall of grey rock leading us. Then I began to notice a variation, just slightly at first, but definitely there. I could just barely make out the top of the slope. As we continued to move, it steadily dropped until it became nothing more than a low fence of rock. In the distance I could see where it dropped away to nothing. I reached up and pulled myself up the side, digging my foot into one of the grooves to get a grip. Buzz did the same thing while Beth ran ahead, climbed up at a lower spot and ran back to join us on the top of the whale.

"Now, we just have to stroll along the back until we reach the highest spot. Don't go too close to the edge," Buzz warned.

This was a warning I didn't need. I hated heights and I wasn't going to get any closer to the edge than I needed to.

"Well?" Beth asked as we started to walk.

"Well, what?" I asked in response.

"Where do you think the treasure is buried?"

"I'm not sure," I reluctantly admitted.

"But you'll figure it out, right?"

"I . . . I guess I will."

"I thought you had everything figured out already," Buzz interjected.

"Not everything . . . like not the exact spot."

"This would be a long walk for nothing," Buzz said.

"And it's not like we can just dig up everything around here," Beth added.

"I know, although from what I can see it can't be right on Humpback Hill."

"Why not?" Beth asked.

"Because this isn't a hill, it's a rock," I said, point-ing out what seemed pretty obvious to me. With the exception of a few sparse pockets of sand and dirt supporting some grass and a couple of dwarfed trees a few feet tall there was nothing to break up the gigantic outcrop of rock.

"He's right," Buzz agreed. "This is solid rock and there's no way he would have tunnelled into this stuff."

"Then where do you think it is buried?" Beth asked.

"Probably somewhere just off to the side of the hill," I said.

"Oh, that's really helpful," Beth said sarcastically.

I wanted to say something back but I knew she was right. Without any other clues we were nowhere. It would take years to dig up the whole area around the hill. We continued to move in silence.

"Is there any point in even going up to the top?" Beth asked.

"What do you mean?"

"If you think it's buried along the base of the hill maybe we should walk around it completely. Maybe there's something on the other side, the one we didn't walk along," she explained.

"I guess that makes sense," I admitted.

"Let's just go on to the top first," Buzz suggested. "It's not far and, like I said, the view is really good from there. Maybe we can sit up there and have lunch. Maybe whatever we're looking for will be visi-ble from the top."

"I guess that might work," Beth agreed.

"We can see everything from up there, even what's going on at the pit."

"That sounds like a good plan to me," I said. Even more important than getting a rest and something to eat and drink, I'd get a chance to think. There had to be something I was missing.

We continued the climb. It wasn't that steep, but it was very rough and there was enough of an incline for my legs to feel the strain. Just when I felt like I needed to rest, the hill flattened out and we were standing along a small level section on the very back of the whale. It continued level for that short section before the edge curved under and out of sight. This was the only flat place on the whole hill.

"This is it," Buzz said. "The highest spot on the whole island."

We peered out at the sights. Just as Buzz had said, we could see way into the distance. Along the shore, like a dark patch on the white sand, sat the village. Out on the bay there were a number of boats, their sails bright against the blue of the water.

There was a strong wind blowing up the face of the cliff and my shirt started to flap noisily. I put a hand on my hat to guard it against being blown away. I backed farther away from the edge. Having a hat blown over the edge would be one thing . . . being blown over the edge a whole different thing.

"From this distance even those gigantic dump trucks look like dinky toys," Buzz said and I turned to look at where he and Beth were staring.

The high yellow fence surrounding the pit stretched out like a ribbon across the sand. Trapped in the centre of the enclosure was a large, black, circular "wound" that had been opened by the diggers and carted away by those trucks. I could make out three trucks, one being loaded and two others bringing their load to be dumped. The asphalt factory belched out smoke that drifted across the sky.

"I wonder how deep they've dug?" I asked.

"It's impossible to tell from here," Beth answered.

"I heard a rumour that they were down almost to the one-twenty mark," Buzz answered. "That puts them within ten feet of the treasure."

"Don't you mean where the treasure is supposed to be?" I asked.

Buzz looked away nervously. Beth looked over at me.

"You don't believe the treasure is here, do you?" I asked.

Buzz shuffled his feet but didn't answer immediately. "I'd like to believe what you're saying, you know, about the treasure being here . . ." He let the sentence trail off to nothing.

"I'm positive it's here!" I protested.

"No offence, Sam . . . it's just that I've lived on this island my whole life and I've heard all about lots of people who were positive they could get the treasure." He shrugged.

I felt a surge of anger that he didn't believe me. I felt like giving him a shot in the face or . . . but what right did I have to be mad at him? My roller coaster ride of emotions had left me in exactly the same place more than once. I'd like to believe, but was far from sure myself.

"Did your rumour tell you how long it's going to be until they dig down to the level where the treasure's *supposed* to be?" I asked.

Buzz didn't argue this time. He shook his head.

"A day or two," Beth answered.

We both turned to her in surprise.

"How do you know that?" I questioned.

"The other night, after you went to bed, I heard Mom and Grandpa fighting. He said he'd prove her wrong in a week or so when they brought up the treasure."

I'd actually still been awake when they started fighting, but I'd pulled the covers over my head so I wouldn't have to listen and snuggled under there with Marmalade.

"That doesn't leave us much time," I said.

"What do you mean?"

"Once they find out the treasure isn't where they think it is then everybody's going to start looking for it in other places. Once we knew to look elsewhere it didn't take us long to figure it out and I doubt it'll take somebody else much time either," I explained.

"So you think we have to find the treasure within a few days?" Buzz asked.

"I really can't say for sure. It could be months before they give up the search at the pit and maybe even longer before somebody looks closely at a map and figures it out."

"So maybe we have a few months," Buzz suggested. "Maybe even longer because nobody else has your *grandfather's* map," he continued.

"But lots of people have seen it," Beth said.

"And maybe even taken pictures of it," I added. "Besides, we don't have that much time. School starts in three weeks. Beth and I will be gone before then."

"That's right," Beth confirmed.

"I could keep looking after you're gone . . . that is if we don't find it before then," Buzz said.

"I wouldn't want to come out here by myself," Beth said.

"Maybe I could ask somebody to help," Buzz suggested.

"No way!" I protested.

"You can't tell anybody else!" Beth agreed. "Nobody, do you understand?"

"Sure . . . okay . . . nobody else."

"Once even one more person finds out then it's no secret. Before you know it everybody who owns a shovel will be up here with it," I said.

"So we have two or three weeks. That should be long enough . . . if we knew where we should dig," Buzz said.

He was right again. If we knew where to dig all we'd need was a day. If we didn't know, it didn't matter whether it was a two-week or a two-year head start, because we weren't going to find anything.

"Maybe we should eat," I suggested.

Beth looked at her watch. "It's almost twelve-thirty."

"No wonder I'm so hungry," Buzz said. "Follow me and I'll show you a spot where we can have lunch."

Buzz led us away from the edge of the cliff. About twenty yards back, right smack in the middle of the rock formation, there was a large depression. I don't know how I missed seeing it when we were coming up. It was five or six paces across, a couple of feet lower than the surrounding rock, and filled with sand. Five sections of a large tree, cut off in sections like stools, sat around the charred remains of a campfire. Somebody had gone to a lot of trouble to get them way up here. Buzz jumped down into the soft sand.

"This is where people sometimes eat when they come up here," he explained. "It's out of the wind and you can get a fire going."

I jumped down and took a seat on one of the stumps. Buzz was right, it was far less windy down here. I took off my backpack and pulled out my water bottle and lunch. Beth and Buzz did the same. A long slurp of water felt good; refreshing even though it had warmed up in the brilliant sunshine.

"You thought about what you might do with your share of the treasure?" Buzz asked Beth.

"A little. You, Sam?"

"Some." It had been what I was thinking about last night as I tried to drift off to sleep.

"And?" Beth asked.

"Well . . ."

"Come on, don't get shy with us. I'm not telling

you what I want to do with my share of the treasure unless you tell us first," Buzz said.

"I was thinking about paying off the house . . . you know, so Mom wouldn't have to work so hard or worry so much."

"Nothing more fun?" Buzz was surprised.

"Not from my brother . . . unless it was to buy some fancy magic tricks."

I wanted to deny it, but she was right.

"Well?" she asked.

"Well, I would like to buy a few props. The kind real magicians use. So what would you do with your share, Buzz?"

"I'd build a bathroom."

I couldn't help but laugh.

"A bathroom? But why?" Beth asked.

"Remember—I grew up with twelve kids in the family, eight of them sisters, and only one bathroom in the house. All my life I've dreamed about what it would be like to go into the bathroom and stay in there as long as I wanted."

"But it must be better now," I said. "Almost all of your brothers and sisters have moved out of the house."

"Moved out, but not left completely. There's always somebody visiting, especially during the summer. And now there's not just eleven of them. They have husbands or wives or boyfriends or girl-friends and kids and . . . you get the idea?"

"I guess so."

"So my fantasy is to have my very own bathroom

added on my bedroom, and nobody would be allowed to use it but me. Sitting on that toilet I'd be like a king on my throne," Buzz said, looking regal.

I tried not to picture what he was talking about but the image popped into my mind.

"And you, Beth?" Buzz asked.

"I don't know," she mumbled.

"I do!" I stated. "Clothes, clothes and more clothes! Right?"

"I was thinking of clothes, but how many clothes do you need?" she asked.

"Judging from the weight of your suitcase I was wondering that myself."

"Shut up!" she snapped. "Is that all you think I'm interested in? Do you think I'm a total airhead?"

"I didn't say that!" I protested. "What else would you do?"

"I was thinking . . . we could fix up Grandpa's house, and pay off his bills and buy that medicine he needs."

"Of course! That goes without saying . . . but I'm glad you said it . . . that's so nice."

"I am a nice person," she said. "Even if I'm not always so nice to you."

"I know," I said.

Beth looked embarrassed. She took a bite from her sandwich and looked away, effectively ending the conversation.

I nibbled on my sandwich. Buzz started rambling on about music videos and Beth happily joined in. I wasn't listening to much they were saying, but the little I did pay attention to sounded like a replay of their last conversation. And the one before that and the one before that.

As I put the wax paper from the sandwich back into my pack, I came across the map. It was neatly folded in two and I'd put it inside a big zip-lock bag to protect it in case my water bottle spilled. I removed the map and took it from the bag. The paper seemed even yellower and the ink more faded under the bright sunlight. The clearest lines were the pencil marks I'd made . . . boy, was I ever going to get into trouble when Grandpa saw those marks. Inside the house they hadn't seemed so bad, but out here in the brilliant sunlight they practically jumped out at you. Actually all the markings were much clearer.

I ran my finger along the lines. There was no denying that all three intersected at the very spot where we sat. I followed one of the lines back to where it came out of the blowhole of one of the whales. There had to be something I was missing. Some little clue.

I brought the map up close to my eyes. There were a few darkened smudges just above the sprays from the whale's blow. Were they just stains or the faded remains of something else? I turned the map to see the second whale and then the third. They all had the same faint smudges. That couldn't be coincidence.

I strained my eyes, trying to make sense of the scattered dots of ink. And then my brain filled in the missing parts. The smudges looked like small coins shooting out of the whales' blowholes.

I leaped to my feet and toppled over the stump I'd

been sitting on. I jumped up onto the surrounding rocks.

"What's wrong?" Beth asked.

"Nothing, nothing's wrong. Buzz, if this wasn't a big rock but a whale, a real whale, where do you think the blowhole would be?"

He chewed lazily on his sandwich, took a drink of water, and swallowed noisily.

"I don't know. Probably around here someplace, I guess."

"No, not around here. Right here! Right where we've been sitting!" I yelled excitedly.

"Yeah, so what?" Beth asked.

I started to laugh and they both looked confused. I tried to contain myself.

"So, if you two can hurry up and finish your lunches we can start digging for the treasure."

"You know where it is?" Beth asked.

"I sure do . . . you're sitting on it."

Chapter Twenty-One

"It's inside this log?" Buzz asked.

So much for thinking that he was smart. "Close. Look at this," I said.

I held up the map for them to see. "Look right here."

"Where?" Beth asked.

"The blowhole of the whale. Can't you see it?"

"See what?" Buzz asked.

"The pieces of eight, streaming out of the blowhole."

They both moved closer to the map and squinted.

"I see something . . . I think," Beth said.

"I just see smudges."

"Either way, so what?" Beth asked.

"Don't you see!" I said excitedly. "The pieces of eight, the treasure, they come right out of the blowhole of the whale and we're sitting directly on top of the blowhole of this whale! It's perfect!" I practically screamed.

There was silence as both Buzz and Beth stared at me in disbelief.

Finally, Buzz spoke. "You mean we're sitting on top of the treasure?"

"Yes."

Buzz and Beth exchanged a smile, a big smile.

"I wonder how deep this goes," Beth said.

"I don't know. The whole rock is covered in holes. Most of them are pretty shallow, but some of the cracks are twice as deep as I am tall, and there's a couple of spots that must be pretty deep because tiny trees are growing out of the sand," Buzz said.

"I guess there's only one way to find out how deep this one is," I suggested.

Beth and Buzz nodded their heads in agreement. Without hearing another word Buzz dropped to his knees and cupped his hands together to scoop out some of the sand. He pitched it up over the side of the depression and onto the rock. Upon reaching the top the grains were captured by the wind and scattered.

I picked up my backpack and pulled out a gardening trowel and two small camping shovels I'd found in the garage.

"Here, try this instead," I said, tossing Buzz one of the shovels.

I handed the second one to Beth. They both started to dig. I gathered up our packs and lifted them off the sand onto the rock. Then I dropped to my knees and started digging as well.

The initial scrambling enthusiasm soon died down. We weren't building a sand castle here but were trying to excavate a hole that was twice as wide in all directions as I was tall. If we had real shovels it might have been different, but as it was we'd been working for almost two hours and had only managed to go down about two feet. Even I wasn't optimistic enough to think Captain Kidd had buried a fortune in gold and jewels only a couple of feet below the surface.

The good news was that the sides of the depression, the solid rock of the hill, seemed to be slanting slightly inwards. That meant that, while we didn't have any idea how deep the depression might go, it was getting narrower as it got there. As well, since we cleared away the sand all the way to the rock sides there was absolutely no danger of anything collapsing on top of us. My one experience of almost drowning in sand was permanently ingrained in my brain and there was no way I was ever going to put myself in a position where that might happen again.

"Let's take a break," Buzz suggested. Nobody argued.

I grabbed my water bottle and took a sip of the small amount of warm water that remained. I was sure neither Beth's nor Buzz's containers held much more. We hadn't thought about bringing more because we hadn't realized how hard we were going to be working or how hot it would get under the cloudless sky. The sun was directly over top of us and the slanting sides of the depression seemed to focus the rays right at us like a magnifying glass. And the very reason we'd originally sat here, to escape from the winds, made the heat even more unbearable. There wasn't even the hint of a breeze and the air just sat there like a thick, hot bowl of oatmeal, pressing against my skin.

Buzz put down his water container and started to chuckle to himself.

"What's so funny?" Beth asked.

"Look at what you're using to dig," he said, pointing to her little shovel.

"It's no worse than yours!" Beth replied.

Buzz held up his shovel. "I didn't say it was. It just strikes me as funny. There they are just a couple of miles away using giant cranes and tractors and dump trucks big enough to hold a dozen cars. And here we are with our . . . toys . . . and it might be us who find the treasure instead of them."

I wasn't thinking about our shovels being compared to the heavy equipment at the Money Pit. Instead I was thinking about Grandpa down with those machines. How he'd dreamed his entire life about finding the treasure and how it wasn't going to be him . . . I felt a tinge of guilt and sadness. If only he could have been here.

The sound of voices being carried by the wind jarred me out of my thoughts. Beth and Buzz heard them too. We dropped our shovels and climbed up so we could see over the rocks. Standing at the edge of the cliff were three people. They were wearing helmets and long-sleeved shirts and pants and had pads around their knees and elbows. They were all staring over the edge.

"Rock climbers," Buzz said, stating the obvious.

"Do you think they've seen us?" I asked.

"Probably not yet, but they might. I watched climbers before and usually they rest at the top before they head back down. I've seen a couple of groups that came right here to eat and have a . . ." A big smile lit up Buzz's face. "To have a drink. Maybe they brought some extra water they can let us have."

I grabbed him by the arm as he started to climb out of the depression.

"Shouldn't we avoid them seeing us?"

"It doesn't matter. Nobody would be able to figure out why we're here. Let's just stash the shovels and we'll go over and say hello."

I hesitated for a minute. It was probably best not to be seen at all, but my craving for water outweighed anything else. And of course Buzz was right, nobody would connect our being there with digging for treasure. We'd dug out a lot of sand but the hole didn't look that much different.

I scooped a little hole in the sand and dropped the three shovels into it. I pushed sand over top so they were covered. There was no point in giving anybody even a little clue. We climbed out of the hole and walked toward them. The rock climbers were so intent on what was going on below—other climbers must have been working their way up the face of the cliff—that they didn't even notice us coming.

"Hi!" Buzz called out.

One of the climbers jumped in surprise and the other two turned our way. There were two men and a woman. All three looked to be in their twenties.

"You startled us," the woman said. "We didn't see any other ropes on the face."

"Did you free climb?" one of the men asked.

"Free climb?" I asked.

"Climb the cliff without ropes," he explained.

"No, of course not. We came up the back way," Beth admitted.

As we talked another climber, a second woman, came over the lip of the cliff and was helped up the last few feet to the top. She looked scared and tired and then surprised when she saw us.

"How did you get up here?" she asked.

"We just walked up," Beth answered.

"You mean you didn't have to climb?"

Beth shook her head.

"And we could get back down that way?" the woman asked.

"Yeah, no problem."

"Well that settles it. There's no way I'm going back down the way I came up!"

"But Jamie!" one of the men objected.

"But Jamie, nothing. You didn't tell me how high this was. I was scared to death coming up and the thing that made it worse was thinking I'd have to go back down the same route. This is like a miracle! Which way do I go, kids?"

"That way," Buzz said, pointing down the back of the whale.

"I'll meet you at the bottom," she said to the man and started to walk away.

"Wait!" the man hollered and she came to a stop. He turned to the other two. "I better go with her. Take all the ropes and things and we'll meet you below."

They nodded in agreement and the man trotted after the woman.

"That may have solved her problem, but it doesn't take care of ours," Buzz said and he too ran after the woman.

He quickly caught up to them and I watched as they talked. She pulled a brightly coloured canteen out of her pack and gave it to Buzz. She and the man turned and continued down the slope as Buzz returned to us.

"Here, take a drink. It's practically full."

I wiped the spout on my shirt and took a drink. It was a thermos-type canteen and the water was still cold. It cooled a trail down my throat and into my stomach. I passed it over to Beth and she took a drink too.

"We better fill our bottles from the canteen so we can get it back to her or her friends," I said.

"Don't bother. She said I could keep it. She mumbled something about it being the least she could give us as a reward for saving her life. She said all she wanted was to get back to town alive."

"That's funny," Beth said.

We sat down on an outcrop of rock and watched as two more people, a man and another woman, climbed up and reached the top of the cliff. They hardly took more than a minute's rest before they started back down.

"That does look like fun," I said.

"I thought you were afraid of heights," Beth said.

"Not afraid . . . just careful."

"They sure were in a hurry to get down," Buzz said as he stood looking over the very edge.

"Maybe we should be doing that too," Beth said. "It must be getting pretty late."

I looked at my watch. "Wow, look at the time! It's almost four o'clock—we should have been back an hour ago! We have to get going."

"But what about the treasure?" Buzz asked.

"It's going to have to wait."

"I guess we can come back with real shovels and maybe some rope and a couple of pails," Buzz said.

"Why rope and pails?" Beth asked.

"When we get deeper we won't be able to toss the sand over the edge. We'll use the rope and pail to haul the sand up," Buzz explained.

"Let's get our stuff and get back to town," I said.

We hurried over to the depression and I jumped down into the sand. I picked up Buzz's pack and tossed it up to him. Next, I did the same with Beth's. I slung mine over my shoulder and went to climb up the side when I remembered about the shovels and stopped.

"Hold on," I said. I dropped to my knees and started pushing away the sand to recover the shovels.

"Just leave 'em," Buzz suggested.

"It'll just take a second," I answered as I pulled the first shovel free of the sand. I quickly located the second and pulled it out. I rummaged around through the sand for the last shovel. It didn't seem to be with the others. I dug down deeper, pushing sand aside with my other hand.

"Come on, Sam, we're going to be in enough trouble without being any later," Beth said.

"I need to find the shovel," I answered.

"Just leave it. We'll get it when we come back tomorrow."

My outstretched fingers, embedded in the sand, hit something solid. I'd found it! I reached down with my other hand and tried to force it to the surface. It seemed stuck . . . and the shape didn't seem right. I pulled harder and as it popped free I fell over, still holding it in my hand. I looked down in shock at what I was holding and dropped it to the sand. I heard Beth scream as I scrambled away from it . . . a bleached white human skull.

Chapter Twenty-Two

I was just getting over the initial shock, and wondering if it really was what I thought it was, when Beth screamed again. Buzz leaped off the rocks and landed almost on top of the skull. With the toe of one shoe he casually tipped it over and it rolled onto its side. He bent down and reached out to touch it.

"What are you doing?" I asked. My voice sounded kind of squeaky.

"Checking it out. I've never seen a real skull before," he answered as he picked it up.

I felt a shudder run down my spine and my feet got a soft and gooey feeling.

"It's definitely a human skull," he said, turning it in his hands to look at all sides.

"Put it down, Buzz," Beth pleaded.

He gave her a questioning look that seemed to ask

why without any words being necessary.

"It's really smooth. Wanna see?" Buzz asked, holding it out for me.

I shook my head vigorously and then thrust my hands behind my back like I was afraid he might hand it to me against my will.

"Leave it Buzz, we have to get going," Beth said.

"We can't just leave it here . . . it's somebody's head."

"You don't understand. I want you to leave it because *it is* somebody's head. You can't just carry around a head!" Beth begged him.

He nodded his head in agreement. "You're right. I can't carry it like this."

That was good—

Buzz reached down and grabbed my backpack. Before I could utter a single syllable he popped the skull into my pack. I took a deep breath and struggled to regain my voice.

"What are you doing?" I demanded.

"Beth was right. I couldn't carry it in my hands and ride my bike so I put it in your bag."

"Then put it in *your* backpack!"

"My pack isn't big enough. It's a pretty big skull."

This was crazy. "I don't want it in my pack. Get it out!"

"I told you it won't fit in my bag and we have to use your pack, unless . . ." Buzz paused and looked up at Beth, holding her bag. "Unless we can use your sister's backpack."

Her eyes grew wide and she shook her head and

clutched her bag tightly to her chest. It was almost reassuring to see that Beth wasn't so goofy that she'd try to impress Buzz by letting him pop the skull into her pack . . . wait a second . . . if she had agreed it would have at least been out of my backpack. Just when I needed her to be goofy she decided to change.

"I guess that settles it," Buzz said.

"That settles nothing!" I shot back. "I want it out of my pack, right now!"

Buzz looked like he was going to argue, but instead a smile creased his face. "If that's what you want, then fine."

"Thanks," I said in relief.

He held my bag out toward me. "If you want it out you take it out."

"But . . . but . . . but," I stammered.

"Or you can leave it in there and I'll carry your pack and you can carry mine. Okay?"

It felt far from okay but I didn't see how I had any option.

We'd travelled off the rock and across the bush to our bikes as fast as we could. Then when we hit the bikes we really motored. Despite all our efforts, though, I knew we were going to be at least two hours late. Maybe that wasn't a big thing for some people, but for Mom, two minutes late was too much. She was always on time and insisted that everybody, especially her kids, be the same way. She claimed she wanted it that way because she was raising us to be "responsible." But I knew, from the sound of her voice and the look in her eyes the few times I had been late, that it had more to do with her worrying and being afraid something had happened to us. I guess I couldn't complain though. I was always very upset when she was late. So I made sure I was always on time. I didn't like to get Mom worried . . . or mad. Beth was a different story though. Not only was she late more than she was on time, but I thought she did it on purpose. Of course, when she did wander in late it usually led to a big fight. My stomach got all nervous just listening to the two of them going at it, but it didn't seem to faze either of them at all.

I was scared of Mom's reaction, but my thoughts rested almost completely on that skull, bouncing up and down in my backpack strapped to Buzz's back. It wasn't just that it spooked me, but what it meant: it was proof we were digging in the right place.

"You were right. All we need is the right tools," I said as I rode up and fell in line beside Buzz and Beth.

"Yeah, three good shovels, a couple of buckets and rope and—"

"I still don't know what the rope is for," Beth said.

Buzz had already explained that.

"To haul the sand up in the buckets. We can't keep throwing it over the side if we go much deeper, and there's no telling how deep we may have to go," Buzz said.

"It could just be another foot or so," I said encouragingly.

"Or it could be another ten feet. And even though

we'll have shovels to speed things up we'll get slower as we have to start hauling the sand up. As we get deeper I figure we won't be able to dig much faster than we did with the little shovels," Buzz explained.

He did seem to have a pretty good idea about all of this digging stuff.

"So ten feet would take us about ten hours," I figured.

"At least, maybe more."

"I'm not looking forward to that. Ten hours under that sun will practically melt us away."

"The way I have it figured, I don't think we have to worry about the sun at all," Buzz said.

"I don't understand."

"What's to understand? The sun always goes down at night."

"Of course, the sun sets at night, but what are you talking . . ." I stopped myself as I answered the question in my head. "We can't go out there at night!"

"It's the only time we *can* go out there. There's too much of a chance of us being seen if we do the digging during the day. I don't want to have to split the treasure more than three ways," Buzz replied.

"We can't go out there at night," I repeated, but louder this time.

"Why?" Buzz challenged me.

"Well . . . for one thing . . . it's dark," I stammered, looking for an answer.

"I'll bring along a big camping lantern. It'll make it as bright as day in the hole."

I pictured what it would be like digging away in a well of light while the entire dark night surrounded us. We wouldn't be able to see anyone, or anything, standing just outside the light staring at us. And even if something wasn't watching us, I knew "somebody" was waiting for us; the headless skeleton was still buried under the sand. I felt a wave of fear, but I didn't want them to know just how scared I felt. There was no way I wanted to go digging there at night.

"Even if we wanted to, we couldn't go," I said. "No way Mom is going to let us go out in the middle of the night. Especially after us being two hours late."

"He's right," Beth confirmed. "There's no point in asking for something like that."

"Who said anything about asking?" Buzz questioned.

"We can't sneak out!" I protested.

"Why not?" he asked.

"Because she doesn't go to bed until really late and—"

"Then we won't leave till late."

"And she gets up early and she'll see we're not there."

"Leave a note. Tell her you two went out early to the beach and you didn't want to disturb her."

"She'll be mad," I said.

"How mad do you think she'll be when you come home with your pack filled with gold?" Buzz asked.

Buzz seemed to have an answer for all my questions.

If only he had an answer to my fears. We rode along in silence for half a minute or so while we all mulled it over.

"Well?" he finally asked.

"I'm in," Beth chimed in.

That was no surprise. Beth smirked at me.

"And you, Sam?"

"I . . . I don't know."

"If he doesn't want to come he doesn't have to," Beth said.

Her defending me surprised me more than finding that skull had and I looked at her in shock.

"If you don't want to come that just leaves more treasure for Buzz and me," she continued.

"More treasure for you two! I'm the one who figured the whole thing out and now you think I don't deserve to get my share of the treasure!"

"Finders keepers, Sam. Come with us and be one of the finders," Beth said.

I didn't answer.

"It figures. Sam is too much of a goodie-two-shoes to come," Beth taunted.

I rode along in silence.

"Little Sammy always does what his Mommy wants and going out at night would make Mommy mad," she continued in a high-pitched voice.

"Shut up, Beth!" I yelled.

"You want me to shut up? Then come with us. Well?"

I pedalled on in silence for a few more seconds. "Count me in," I grunted through clenched teeth. What choice did I have? Apprehensive or scared, I had to go.

"Good! How about we meet behind your garage at around two in the morning?" Buzz asked.

"Mom may still be awake."

"Then I'll wait until you get there. And don't worry about any of the tools. I'll bring everything."

The rest of the ride was accomplished in silence. I didn't think it was just me who was contemplating what we'd committed ourselves to doing. It wasn't just scary, but insane! It was the sort of thing Grandpa would do. I smiled. Yeah, like Grandpa.

I felt more comfortable as we reached town and finally turned onto Grandpa's street. Buzz suddenly skidded to a stop and I almost slammed into him as I brought my bike to a halt.

"Why did you do that?" I demanded as Beth stopped beside us.

"Look," he said, pointing to Grandpa's house.

There in front of it was a police car.

"I wonder why the Sheriff would be here?" Buzz asked.

"I don't know," Beth said in alarm. "I hope nothing's happened to—"

"Something did happen," I said, interrupting her.

"What do you mean?" she asked.

"Us. We happened. We're two hours late and Mom's reported us missing."

"Come on, that can't be true," Buzz scoffed.

"He's right. You don't know our mother," Beth disagreed as she started her bike back in motion. My heart was pounding as hard as my feet were pumping on the pedals as Buzz and I followed after her. We caught up as she came to a stop right in front of the house.

"Well?" I asked.

"We have to go in. We'll only be in bigger trouble the longer we wait," Beth replied.

"Good luck. I'll meet you two behind your garage at two," Buzz said. "Oh, and here."

Before I could react Buzz took my pack off his back and slung it over the end of my handle bars.

"What are you doing!"

"Giving you back your pack."

"But you said—"

"That I'd carry it home. You're home."

"But . . . but . . ."

"And I'll take my pack," Buzz said as he reached over and took it from me. "See you later," he called over his shoulder as he rode away. It looked like Buzz was going to get away scot free. So much for us being a team.

I looked over at Beth helplessly.

"Let's get inside," she said.

"But what about the skull?"

"Leave it out here."

"I can't just leave it here!" I protested.

"Would you rather bring it in and show the policeman?" Beth asked.

"No! Of course not!"

"Besides, if I were you, I wouldn't be so worried about *that* dead guy."

"What do you mean?" I asked.

"Think about it," she said as she set her bike down on the sandy ground.

I did, and I knew what she meant. The dead guys I should be worrying about were me and her, when Mom saw us.

Chapter Twenty-Three

I heard the yelling before we got to the door and my stomach did a flip. We'd have to find a whole lot of treasure to make up for this. The loudest voice sounded like Grandpa. I could understand why Mom would be mad, that was sort of like her, but I couldn't understand him being so upset. Maybe he was defending us. I looked over at Beth and her face was a mirror of the fear I was feeling. She couldn't even pretend to be cool. This was more upsetting to me than finding the skull. She took a deep breath and opened the door. I followed in behind, using her as a shield. Maybe they'd be madder at Beth because she was older.

Instantly, the angry voices became louder and sharper. It was Grandpa and Mom. I stopped and Beth reached back and took me by the hand to lead me down the hall. We walked into the room and the two of them and a police officer were so engaged in their discussion that they didn't notice us. Beth cleared her throat, but they didn't hear her over the raised voices.

"Hello," she called out tentatively.

Mom looked over and nodded her head, but didn't say a word. They continued to argue.

"We're home, Mom," I said. "Sorry we're a bit late."

"Not now, Sam," she answered.

Not now? What was going on here?

"I'm sorry, Mr. Simmons," the Sheriff said firmly. He was a big man and his gun and hat made him look even bigger. "But I have no choice."

"You're lucky I'm not twenty years younger or you'd have no *teeth*!" Grandpa yelled.

Why was he threatening the Sheriff? Was the guy going to do something to us and Grandpa was protecting us? That would be just like him and probably explained why he and Mom were yelling as well.

"I'm just doing my job," he replied calmly.

"Since when is it your job to take away a man's driver's licence when he hasn't done anything wrong?"

Driver's licence . . . what was going on here? I looked over at Beth. It was obvious from her expression that she didn't understand things any better than I did.

"I'm just following the law. The doctor ordered your licence suspended while he conducts a full examination to determine your mental status," the officer explained.

"This isn't right! I fought in the war to preserve our freedom and you two little boys, one of you playing doctor and the other pretending he's a cop, are trying to ruin my life! I wouldn't let him examine my dog, and as for you, you aren't fit to be a meter reader!" Grandpa screamed.

"He's a real doctor and I'm a real cop," the Sheriff answered softly.

I was amazed at how calm he was. Not only was Grandpa yelling but he was practically on top of the guy, so close that as he screamed little bits of his spit landed on the officer's face.

"Now get out of my house before I toss you out!" Grandpa bellowed.

"I'll leave . . . when you give me your licence and—"

"Tell him he can't have my licence, Rebecca! Tell him I'm a good driver!" Grandpa pleaded.

She didn't answer, but instead looked away.

"Tell him! Tell him!"

"I . . . I can't," Mom said softly. She looked like she was on the verge of tears.

"What do you mean you can't?" Grandpa's voice was barely a whisper.

"I can't because . . ."

"Because what?"

". . . because I think what he's doing is right."

I held my breath and waited for the explosion.

Grandpa opened his mouth, but he didn't answer. He looked . . . looked . . . defeated.

"You want my licence," he said quietly. "Well, here it is." Grandpa reached into his back pocket and took it out of his wallet.

The officer reached out for it, but Grandpa dropped it to the floor. Slowly, the officer bent down and picked up the piece of paper.

"Now get out," Grandpa hissed.

"I have a few more things to take care of first," the officer replied.

"Fine, you stay and I'll leave."

"You can't leave!" Mom objected loudly.

"What are you talking about?" he asked.

"Dr. Robinson is coming back around to complete his examination and—"

"One *more* reason to leave. I'm gone," Grandpa said. He started for the door.

Mom turned to the officer. "Can't you make him stay?" she pleaded.

Grandpa stopped at the door. He wanted to know the answer to that question too.

He shook his head. "I can only stop him from driving. Mr. Simmons, are you going to be driving?"

"That's none of your . . ." He paused. "No, I'm going out for a walk . . . a long walk. Do you have anything else you want to try to take away from me?"

Again the officer shook his head.

"Good. I've lost enough today. My licence, my dignity . . . and my daughter."

He turned and left the house. The overwhelming silence was finally broken as Mom burst into tears and ran from the room. I took a step to follow when Beth grabbed my arm to stop me.

"Leave her alone . . . for a minute. She needs to be alone," Beth said, and I knew she was right.

Chapter Twenty-Four

There was a lot we *could* have talked about, and almost as much we *should* have talked about, but we didn't. Instead, we moved around the house, pretending what had happened really hadn't, and that we weren't listening for the front door to open and for Grandpa to come back in. He didn't come back. Not after supper or that evening or by the time we went to bed.

Both Beth and I went to our rooms, as agreed, earlier than usual, so we could get at least a little bit of rest even if we didn't get any sleep. I wanted to call the whole thing off but Beth wouldn't hear anything about that. She said she was going, with or without me.

I lay in bed listening. I could hear the sounds of the wind rustling through the trees and Mom moving around the house. What I didn't hear was the front door opening or the sound of Grandpa's voice. For once in my life I would have been relieved to hear the two of them arguing. He hadn't come home and I didn't think he would. Since he knew practically everybody on the island, I figured he'd have no problem finding a place to stay tonight. Maybe it was even better this way. Both he and Mom would have a chance to calm down. They both needed some time apart before they said anything more they'd only regret.

I was surprised when I heard her move into her bedroom just after one in the morning. That was early for her to turn in. Finally, after I hadn't heard any sounds for fifteen minutes, I climbed out of my bed and crept to the door of my room. There were still lights on in the hall and the living room, probably left on for Grandpa, but her bedroom door was closed and there was only darkness showing under the door. There was nothing to do but wait. I climbed back into bed and pulled the covers over me. Marmalade almost instantly took his place on my chest. I liked the feel of his warmth against me. Maybe I should just go back to sleep until . . . the map! I'd forgotten about the map. It was sitting out in the front yard in my backpack along with that skull. What if somebody picked it up? What if it rained? What if it got totally ruined by the dew overnight? That map meant so much to Grandpa and now it just lay outside. He'd already had so many bad things happen to him . . . But could I go outside by myself at night to retrieve a map that was sitting alongside a human skull?

There was no point in thinking it through any further or trying to convince myself one way or another. I had no choice. I had to go and get it. Gently, I pushed Marmalade off my chest and threw my legs over the side of the bed. Silently, I grabbed my slippers from the drawer and on slippered feet I padded out of my room and down the hall. The light made me feel exposed, but at least I was able to see clearly and there was no danger of me bumping into anything and waking Mom up.

I stepped out into the night air, noiselessly closing the door behind me. I couldn't take a chance since Mom might still be half-awake, listening for the sound of the front door. The air was cool and fresh. The house had been aired out so well and the kitty litter tended to so carefully that it didn't smell that bad in the house anymore, but outside still smelled better.

Within a few steps my feet became caked with sand, wet from the dew. I hoped none of the dew had seeped through the pack and gotten through the flap of the plastic bag and damaged the map.

The moon was hidden behind thick clouds and I could just make out the outline of the bikes lying on the sand. I could picture all sorts of things hidden in the shadows that surrounded me. Getting closer I could see the pack there beside the bikes. As I reached down to pick it up my mind was flooded with images; here I was, all by myself, in the middle of the night, under a dark sky, getting ready to pick up a human skull. I froze.

"What are you doing, Sam?"

I jumped into the air and spun in the direction of the voice. I wanted to scream, but it got stuck in my throat and only a frightened gurgle escaped.

"What are you doing out here at this time?"

It was Grandpa! I could just make out his outline intertwined with that of the chair he was sitting in.

"I . . . I was just getting my pack . . . I forgot it out here," I explained. I grabbed it by one of the straps and lifted it up. The shock seemed to have driven out my fear of picking up the skull.

Slowly, I walked toward him. "What are you doing out here?" I asked.

"Thinking. Just thinking."

"Maybe you should come in. It feels like it might rain."

He shook his head. "No rain tonight. It's just mist off the water."

"Aren't you cold?"

"I feel a chill right through me, but it doesn't have a thing to do with the temperature. You better be going in, though."

Part of me wanted to go inside, but the biggest part of me knew I couldn't just walk away from him.

"Would it be all right if I stayed out here with you for a while?" I asked.

"You should go inside. But *I* don't force people to do things they don't want to do or . . . that would be nice. Pull up a chair."

I grabbed one of the chairs that were leaning against the low stone fence and pulled it up next to him. I sat down and waited for him to say something. He remained silent and I struggled to think of what I could say.

"I'm sorry about your licence."

"So am I."

"But it doesn't have to be gone for long," I said hopefully. "You can see the doctor tomorrow and convince him that you're okay. I know you can."

He let out a low, soft chuckle and took one of my hands in his. It felt warm and safe in his hand and I couldn't help thinking back to all the years he'd taken me by the hand and helped me cross the street, or kept me safe from the waves as we played in the surf, or showed me the right way to hold a bat or . . .

"I won't be getting it back," he said finally.

"But there's nothing wrong with you—"

"Sshhhhhh," he said as he gave my hand a gentle squeeze. "A dozen years before your sister was born my father passed on. Do you know anything about my Papa?"

"He was a sea captain, right? I've seen his picture in Mom's album."

"You're right. He was a captain. A great captain. He knew all there was to know about sailing and the creatures that live in the ocean. And more than that he knew about people and countries and history and he always had a funny story or a joke to tell."

"He sounds like you," I said.

Again his gentle chuckle filtered through the night air. "And I used to think that he was just about the smartest man I ever knew . . . that is, until the final years of his life. Do you know what it means to be senile?"

I shook my head.

"It's something that happens to a lot of old people. They become more and more forgetful and they lose track of things."

That sounded like the disease Dr. Robinson was talking about.

"They can even become dangerous to themselves because they don't know what's happening around them. That's what happened to my dad. In the end he hardly knew his name. He didn't know who I was . . ." His voice caught and I could hear the tears hidden behind the words. "Saddest days of my life were watching that man, that proud determined man, reduced to almost . . . to almost nothing . . . and that's what's happening to me."

"It's not! You're just a little forgetful! Everybody forgets things sometimes! I know I forget things, like notes from the teacher or to practice the piano or—".

He reached out and gently placed a finger against my lips to silence me. "I thank you for what you're trying to do, Sam, I really do." There was a long pause. "Did I ever tell you the proudest day of my life?"

I shook my head.

"It happened just over eleven years ago."

"Around the time I was born," I said.

"The day you were born. Your mother called me on the phone to tell me that I had a grandson and that the two of you were fine. And she told me she was calling you Samuel, naming you after me . . . because she hoped you'd grow up to be the man I was . . . can you imagine that."

I could. I was always so proud that I was named after him.

"But I don't understand . . . you remember that so well and that was so long ago," I said.

"I always remember the olden days."

"But what about the way you fixed your truck!"

"Some things, like fixing the truck, haven't been affected at all. And it's funny but some of those things from the old days I even remember better than before. I've been remembering things from when I was a kid. Things I'd forgotten about or haven't thought of for years. Those thoughts come flooding back all the time. Mostly happy memories. Meeting your grandmother, your mother as a little girl, my first car, trips and vacations."

He chuckled and a big smile pushed its way through the stubble and wrinkles on his face. Then the smile faded away. "But then I forget things I should know. For the life of me I can't remember your mother's middle name, or where I put my glasses, and a couple of times I parked my truck in town and I had to wander around because I couldn't remember where I left it."

"But what about the Money Pit? Nobody knows more about it than you."

"It's old stuff, like the truck." He shook his head sadly. "Besides, it turned out that nothing I thought I knew was right."

"What do you mean?" I asked.

"I guess it won't be secret for very much longer so I might as well tell you. We reached the level where the treasure was supposed to be four days ago."

"Maybe you just have to go deeper," I said, although I don't know why. There was no point in digging another ten or ten thousand feet.

"We did continue digging, twenty feet lower than we should have, but we found all we're going to find."

"You found something?"

"Five wooden chests."

My heart soared and sank at the same time. "You found the treasure?"

"We found the treasure chests, but there was no treasure. All they held were rocks. I couldn't believe it when we broke open that first chest. Rocks, nothing but rocks."

Buzz had been right about the rocks!

Grandpa shook his head slowly. "It was all just a joke, just a big two-hundred-year-old joke that fooled thousands of people, although maybe nobody as badly as me. I've lost everything. Everything. My life savings, my house. Everything." His voice had dropped off until it was nothing more than a faint whisper.

I felt my tongue grow thick and my chin started to shake. "It's going to be okay, Grandpa. Everything will be okay."

He gave my hand another squeeze. "I wish I could see how."

I got up from the chair and sank to my knees on the sand in front of him. "Could you do something for me, Grandpa?"

"Anything for you, Sam, anything."

"Come treasure hunting with me . . . tonight."

Chapter Twenty-Five

"It's too late and I'm too tired, and even if we wanted to the guards wouldn't let me bring you to the pit," Grandpa said.

"I'm not talking about the pit."

"Then what?" he asked.

"I want you to come with me to where the treasure is buried."

"Thanks for what you're trying to do," Grandpa said. "I know you're trying to cheer me up."

"It's not that. I know where the treasure is buried and we were planning on going out to get it tonight."

"We? You mean you and Beth?"

"And Buzz. We're going out to dig up Captain Kidd's treasure . . . tonight."

He shook his head. "You three are planning on sneaking out tonight?"

"Yes. We're meeting him soon."

"And just where are you going?" he asked.

"To where the treasure is buried. We know where the treasure is, honest!"

Grandpa got up from the chair and I stood up as well. "I've wasted my life chasing something that was nothing more than a ghost. Don't waste your life running after rumours and shadows. Come on, let's get to bed," he said.

"Bed! But you don't understand, we can't go to bed. We're going to dig up the treasure. Beth and I are meeting Buzz at two o'clock and he's bringing shovels and a lantern and we're going to get the treasure!"

"Not tonight you're not. We're going in the house and you're going to bed."

"You can't! You have to let us go!" I protested.

"There's no way I'm letting my grandkids wander out of my house in the middle of the night on some sort of wild goose chase. If I did I'd be as batty as they think I am."

"But . . ." I realized that he didn't believe me, but why should he? He'd spent his entire life believing one thing and I was asking him, in a few seconds, to change all of it.

"Wait, just a second. Let me show you," I said.

I bent down and gently set my pack on the ground. I undid the buckle and carefully, so my hand didn't even brush up against the skull, reached in and pulled out the baggy that contained the map.

"The treasure wasn't in the Money Pit," I started to say.

"Somebody must have beat us to it."

"No, it never was in the pit. The pit was just a trick to keep people looking in the wrong place. I'll show you where the money is," I said as I removed the map from the bag.

"My map. What's it doing in your pack?"

"I brought it with us today. It gave me the clues to show where the treasure is really buried. Here, look."

I held the map out to him.

"The secret is with these three whales," I said.

"You mean the ones that are different from the rest?"

I was startled, but then realized that of course he knew everything about the map so there shouldn't be any surprise.

"Look, I drew lines joining the three spouts. "

"You did what?" he said abruptly.

"I drew some lines . . . I used a pencil . . . they'll rub off . . . but that isn't important."

"How can it not be important? About the only thing I own of any value is this map and you drew all over it!"

"I didn't draw all over it, look! Just three lines. I had to do it to find the treasure."

He opened his mouth to answer but he didn't. He was staring at the map and his fingers traced the faint path of one of the pencil lines.

He looked up at me. "They meet at Humpback Hill don't they?"

I nodded my head.

"And you think the treasure is up there by the hill?"

"We think we know exactly where it is," I said softly.

"So did I, but I was pretty darned wrong."

"But we found something!" I protested.

Even in the dim, thin light I saw his brow furrow.

"It's right here in my bag."

I reached down and picked up the pack. I passed the whole thing to him so I wouldn't have to handle the skull myself. I wanted to warn him, but I didn't know what exactly to say. He reached in and casually, like he was just picking up a melon, took out the skull. He turned it around just like Buzz had done earlier so he could look at it from all angles.

"Where did you find it?"

"Up on Humpback Hill. Right where we're digging for the treasure."

"It's old."

"Two hundred years old," I suggested.

"Not necessarily. It could be older or younger. Who knows where it came from."

"From Captain Kidd. It's a member of his crew."

"Sam, people have been living on this island for thousands of years. Who knows who this was?"

"It's got to be from his crew. Why else would it be right there?"

"Maybe just a coincidence," he offered. "Um . . . did you notice this?" he asked, holding the skull out to me.

"Notice what?"

"The whole skull is clean and smooth. So smooth you could use it as a bowl and pour in your cereal and milk. Except the milk would run out right here," he said, pointing to a dark line. "The skull was fractured. Looks like something smashed against this man's head. Could have been what killed him."

"Dead men tell no tales," I said.

"What?"

"Dead men tell no tales. Isn't that what you always told me? He was killed so he couldn't tell anybody where the treasure was really buried."

Grandpa looked down at the map. I started to say something, but he "ssshhhed" me. I watched in silence as the seconds ticked away. Then it crossed my mind that maybe he was really thinking about what I'd told him, and the longer he thought the more he'd realize just how right I was and . . .

"You better get in the house now," he said.

My soaring hopes crashed to the ground. He hadn't believed a word I'd said. What would Beth say when she found out I'd blown it? I shouldn't have told him anything, but I'd felt like I had to.

"It's almost two o'clock. Be real quiet when you get your sister. I'll meet the two of you down by the garage."

Chapter Twenty-Six

I stood there with my mouth wide open and watched Grandpa disappear into the darkness. His words echoed around my brain: "Be quiet when you get your sister and I'll meet the two of you down by the garage." He believed me and he was coming with us!

I hurried into the house, moving as quietly as I could. Just as I got near Beth's bedroom door it opened and she popped her head out. I think me standing there startled her as much as her popping out had thrown me and I could tell she looked a little flustered and a lot nervous. I thought we both did well not to scream out in surprise.

As she came out of the room I noticed she was already wearing a thick sweater and was carrying her shoes. I'd felt chilled standing outside in just my T-shirt with Grandpa and I motioned for her to wait while I went back into my room and retrieved my denim jacket. Beth was anxiously waiting by the front door and I scooped my shoes off the shelf by the door and carried them outside. I kicked off my slippers. I was still carrying my pack in my other hand. She followed, closing the door softly behind her.

"Are you scared?" she asked in a hushed tone as we started for the garage.

"A little. You?"

She nodded. I didn't know if I found it reassuring or not that Beth was frightened.

I thought I better tell her about the extra person joining our trip before she bumped into Grandpa in the night. Nothing came to mind and we only had a few dozen more steps before we'd be at the garage. There was nothing to do but spit it out.

"Grandpa is coming."

She skidded to a stop in front of me and I bumped into her.

"Where is he?" she asked.

"Down by the garage."

"Then we better hide," she said.

"No, you don't understand . . . he's in the garage, waiting for us. He's coming with us."

"What did you say?"

"I invited Grandpa to come with us."

"You did what?"

"Invited him to come with us," I repeated.

"Are you crazy?" she exclaimed.

"No . . . and neither is he . . . I had to invite him . . .

he needed to come with us," I said softly. "And I think we need him too."

I wasn't sure if she understood what I said. I wasn't even sure if I completely understood it myself, but I knew it was right. Grandpa had to be part of finding the treasure.

"Come on, he's waiting," I said, and started back down the path.

Rounding the corner of the garage I saw Buzz and Grandpa loading things into the back of the truck. Buzz waved.

"Climb in," Grandpa announced.

"You can't drive, they took away your licence," I said.

"Yeah, but they should have taken away my keys," he laughed as he waved them in front of us.

"But you're not supposed to drive," I argued.

"I sure as heck ain't going to ride a bike out to Humpback Hill. Let's go."

"But what if we get stopped by the police?" I asked.

"What's the worst they can do? They already took my licence."

"But . . ."

"But nothing. I'm driving. And unless you can pedal fast enough to keep up with me, you better get in the truck."

We circled around to the passenger door.

"I hope you don't mind us inviting him," I whispered to Buzz.

"No way. We get a ride and another person to help dig."

Beth climbed in first, followed by Buzz. I got in last and pulled the door closed with a loud slam.

"Sorry," I apologized, remembering Mom asleep in the house.

Grandpa started the engine up. It sounded awfully loud in the silence of the night. He backed it out of the garage and then we started slowly rolling along the alley.

"Did you leave Mom a note?" I asked.

"No. I thought you did."

"I forgot. Maybe we should go back."

"There's no going back. You're both in deep trouble with or without a note," Grandpa pointed out.

He pulled out of the alley and we started down the street. The houses were all dark and the few scattered street lights cast only dim haloes. There wasn't another car on the road. My eye was caught by movement and I saw a skunk ambling down the side of the road, taking his time like he owned the town. Then again, at two in the morning he probably did.

We came to a rolling stop at the corner and turned onto the main street. We had no choice but to drive right through town. I didn't like that, but I was relieved to see there wasn't any traffic along here, either. Grandpa accelerated and the breeze felt good as it flowed in through the open windows.

As we neared the hotel there were cars parked along both sides of the street and a few clumps of noisy people strolling along the sidewalk. We passed by the hotel and I saw the flare of headlights and a car pulling out from the alley. I looked back through the window and tried to see the car, but I couldn't make out anything except the glare of the lights. I felt the truck gain speed and watched the headlights fade farther behind. Then, just as quickly as the lights receded, they started to gain on us until they were only a half dozen car lengths behind again. I felt sweat start to trickle down my side. We passed the last store on the main drag and began passing scattered houses. Grandpa pushed the truck to go faster and once again we left the lights farther behind. I didn't know who was behind those lights but it was good to see them fade away. They'd probably turn into one of those houses and . . . my heart jumped into my throat as red flashing lights suddenly beamed out from the car.

"Darn it!" Grandpa cursed loudly.

"What's wrong?" Beth questioned.

"We got company."

"Company? What do you mean company?" Beth asked. She hadn't seen the lights.

"Police company, right behind us," Grandpa replied.

Beth and Buzz scrambled around in the seat to look at the police car closing in on us.

"What are we going to do?" Beth asked anxiously.

"We have no choice," Grandpa said as he eased the truck over to the side.

My heart sank. We were finished before we'd hardly started.

A cloud of dust erupted behind us, partially obscuring the flashing lights. We rolled to a stop and the police car pulled to a stop behind us.

"Hey, Sam, can you make a policeman disappear?" Grandpa asked.

"What?" What was he talking about? He was going to be arrested and we'd all have to face our mother—I figured I'd rather go to jail.

"Can you do a magic trick to make a policeman disappear?"

I shook my head. Everything he'd said this evening had all made such sense and now he was rambling on about magic. I watched the policeman get out of his car and start to walk toward us.

"Well, I can't make a policeman disappear either," Grandpa said, "But I sure can make a police *car* disappear. Hold on."

Grandpa put the truck back into gear. The engine roared as he pushed down on the gas pedal and the truck rocketed backwards. My neck snapped back as the truck smashed into the police car with a sickening crash!

Chapter Twenty-Seven

Grandpa slammed the car into drive and we squealed away from the squad car, pelting it with a hail of gravel thrown up by our tires. I looked back. The whole front end of the car was smashed and along with the still-flashing lights there was steam erupting from under the crushed and bent hood! As I watched, the officer, who had thrown himself onto the pavement away from the on-rushing truck, picked himself up. He shook a fist at us. The truck fish-tailed back and forth as the tires gripped the pavement.

"Wow!" Buzz exclaimed.

"Grandpa, what did you do?" Beth yelled out in disbelief.

My mouth opened and my mind raced with things I wanted to scream, but no words came out.

"Like I told you, I made a police car disappear.

What do you think, Sam, is that a good magic trick or what?" he cackled.

"Um . . . um . . . um . . ." I stammered, still trying to recover from the shock of what he had done. This couldn't be real. None of this could have just happened. It was like watching a movie or a bad dream or—

"You can't just go smashing into police cars," Beth screamed.

"Not police *cars*, police *car*," Grandpa said. "There was only one of them and it isn't like I make a habit out of this. 'Sides, it was the only way I could figure to get away. I spent my whole life dreaming about that treasure and I'm not going to stop now."

"But you're going to be in gigantic trouble!" Beth argued.

"Already in trouble, remember they took my licence away."

"They'll do more than that. They could put you in jail!"

"Jail? What makes you think they'll put me in jail?"

"You just destroyed a police car!" Beth screamed.

"Yeah, I guess that would make the Sheriff a bit testy, but it'll all be forgiven when I buy 'em a new car."

"But I thought you didn't have any money," I said, proud that I finally managed to say something.

"I don't . . . I invested everything I had in the Money Pit."

"Then where are you going to get the money?" Buzz asked.

"Yeah, you don't have any money," I repeated.

He looked over at Buzz and me with a quizzical look on his face. "Isn't that what we're supposed to be going out to find, a treasure worth a whole lot of money?"

"Well, yeah."

"And don't I get a share of the treasure?"

"Of course," I answered. "Equal partners. One quarter of everything we find belongs to you."

Grandpa reached across Beth and Buzz and patted me on the leg.

"Now, can you explain all of this a little bit more?" he asked. "I couldn't quite follow everything you told me."

"Sure," I said. I couldn't believe he'd come along without understanding every last little detail of what we were doing. I repeated a lot of what I'd already told him and then added on some extra details.

"All makes sense to me," Grandpa said. "I just hope you're right."

"So do I." I was thinking about what was riding on my theory. It wasn't just Beth and Buzz being mad at me or a lost night's sleep. We'd rammed a police car! My Grandpa, on the strength of my theory, was risking everything. What if I was wrong?

"But how did he get the treasure up to Humpback Hill?"

"I think Captain Kidd took it out there little bit by little bit. Probably with a couple of men helping him," I continued.

"And you think that fella in your backpack was one of those helpers?"

"I think it had to be somebody—"

"You better slow down," Buzz interrupted. "The place where we head off the road is just up ahead."

"We're not stopping there," Grandpa answered.

"Then where are we going?" I asked in alarm. Was he okay?

"About half a mile down the way."

"But why?" I asked. It didn't make any sense to walk farther than we had to.

"There's only a few roads on the whole island. By this time Gus, he's the officer who had that little 'accident' back there, has contacted the Sheriff and they're starting to come after us. So to slow 'em down we have to use some of that hocus-pocus stuff. Just like the magic you do."

"What do you mean?" I asked.

"We have to get them looking in the wrong place. This is far enough," he said as he pulled the truck off to the side of the road. "We get out here and it looks like we were going to the pit. Isn't that where every-body figured we were going anyway?"

"I guess so."

Grandpa climbed out of the truck and we all scrambled out the other door.

"But if they think we went to the Money Pit, why would the truck be left here?" I asked.

"Because I got a flat tire," he answered. Grandpa pulled a knife out of his pocket and plunged it into one of the tires, allowing a flood of air to rush out. I watched in shock as the air escaped and the back of the truck sagged down.

"And the spare tire was flat as well," he said. He bent down and thrust the knife into the spare and air hissed free. "They'll think they were both damaged in the crash. Now the three of you walk that way," he said, pointing into the bush.

"But Humpback Hill is the other—"

"I know which way it is," Grandpa interrupted, "but I want you to walk that way. Kick up some dust, knock down some plants. Go till you hit a little stream about seventy paces or so. Then I want you to come back, and here's the important part. When you come back, I want you to walk *backwards*."

"Walk backwards? Why would we . . ." Buzz started to question.

"Come on!" I exclaimed. "I understand and I'll explain it to you."

I started off and Beth and Buzz rushed to catch up to me.

"Is he losing it?" Beth asked.

"No. His mind is working great . . . better than yours," I taunted. "We're doing this to throw them off. We're setting a trail they can follow in the wrong direction. When they get to the creek they'll think we walked along in the water for a while and they'll have to check upstream and downstream to look for us."

"It's like in a movie I saw," Buzz added. "These guys escaped from prison and to get away from the bloodhounds they walked into the river."

"Bloodhounds! Come on, let's not get dramatic. It's not like they'll send dogs after us," Beth said.

"They could," Buzz said.

"Yeah, right," Beth said under her breath.

That was more like the Beth I knew.

"I don't know about dogs, but people could follow tracks. There's the creek," I said, pointing ahead.

We walked right up to the mud and then started to carefully walk backwards. It was important that our tracks only showed us going in one direction; away from the truck and toward the Money Pit. It was awkward, moving backwards in the dark over the uneven ground, and we had to move slowly to stop from falling over. By the time we got back to the truck Grandpa had already unloaded the equipment right on the road. Spread out on the pavement were three long shovels, two pails, a coil of rope, a big lantern and a tarp.

"Okay, we did it," I said.

"Good. Now everybody grab some of the stuff."

Grandpa grabbed a pail, the lantern and a shovel. I wanted to say something, maybe take some of what he was carrying, but he seemed okay, and I wouldn't know how to say anything without offending him anyway. Besides, I had no idea how we would have carried the stuff out here if Grandpa and his truck hadn't come along.

"I want everybody to walk right down the centre of the road, single file," Grandpa said.

"Shouldn't we walk on the side of the road?" I asked.

"Not tonight. If we walk down the middle of the road we won't be leaving tracks and our scent will be burned off before noon."

"What do you mean 'our scent'?" Beth asked.

"Our smell. Once they find out we're not where they think we are, they're going to put together a search party. Probably fly some dogs over from the mainland."

"Bloodhounds?" Buzz asked.

"Yep, they did that last year to find a missing kid."

Buzz turned to face Beth. "Bloodhounds."

She didn't utter a word, but her expression said everything.

"But this way by the time the dogs arrive our smell should be gone," Grandpa explained. "Come on."

We fell in behind him. He was setting a tremendous pace and I struggled under the weight of the bucket and shovel to keep up. I was pleasantly surprised by his energy. I hadn't seen him move this quickly the entire time we'd been here, and Beth and Buzz were even falling behind as we went.

Grandpa muttered something under his breath.

"What's wrong?" I asked.

"I left my glasses in the truck. Always leaving something somewhere and there isn't any time to go back and get them." He turned around. "Buzz, get up here and show me the place we should leave the road!"

Buzz came clanging up and Beth scrambled to get up with us as well.

"Anywhere along here is good," Buzz said.

"Okay, then right here," Grandpa said as he started for the side of the road.

"Um . . . Grandpa . . . it's the other way," I said,

pointing off to where Humpback Hill was located in the darkness.

He looked momentarily confused and then nodded his head and walked back toward us.

"Look back there!" Buzz yelled.

Down the road, still well in the distance, we saw the glare of headlights punctuated by pulsing flashes of red. It was the police and they were coming . . . for us.

"Everybody off the road!" Grandpa yelled.

I jumped slightly in shock and then froze.

"Come on, move it Sam!" Beth called.

I looked over. Beth and Buzz and Grandpa were already off to the side. I unfroze and started to move, but as I did I dropped the pail and then kicked it with my foot as I bent to pick it up. It skittered away a couple of feet. I finally grabbed hold of it. I looked down the road. The car had closed the distance amazingly fast, although its lights were still only illuminating a stretch of road well away from me.

"Move it, you idiot!" Beth screamed.

I scrambled off the road, down the sandy shoulder and into the bordering bushes.

"What were you waiting for, to become road kill?" Beth asked.

Before I could answer I heard the engine of the car whining out. We both turned toward the road. The sound of the motor got louder and louder and louder and then the pavement right in front of us was lit by the approaching headlights. Like a bullet, the car shot by our hiding spot, pushing aside a whoosh of wind that I could feel against my face.

"It's amazing how fast you can drive when you're mad enough," Grandpa chuckled. "We better get going."

"But what about the tracks we just left?" I asked.

"Yeah, we should do something," Grandpa conceded.

"I've got an idea," Beth said. She went out of the bushes and slowly walked right up to the edge of the road. The police car, which was well down the way, flashed its brake lights. For a second I thought that somehow they'd seen her and were coming back, but then I realized they'd probably just reached the truck. Beth started to use the back of the shovel to smooth out our footprints so there was no trace of us leaving the road. She finished and rejoined us in the bushes.

"Let's go treasure hunting," she said.

Chapter Twenty-Eight

Buzz had brought along two flashlights as well as the big lantern, but Grandpa wouldn't let us use them. He said there was no telling how the light would bounce around or show up in the night sky. Of course he was right, but that didn't make it any easier as we stumbled over the broken ground, scattered rocks and bushes. After we'd tramped along for about thirty minutes the clouds opened up slightly and bright beams of moonlight helped to illuminate the path.

As we moved, I kept one eye on the path and the other on Grandpa. He was starting to slow down and I wondered how long he could move at this pace. Or for that matter, how long any of us could go without a break. Grandpa was surprising me. Not just the way he was moving, but the way he'd been thinking all of this through. Sure he had started to go the wrong way off the road, but he was doing okay . . . actually better than okay.

We twisted and turned as we moved and I was beginning to think we'd gotten ourselves lost. I wanted to ask, but I was afraid of both the answer and breaking the silence. Nobody had said a word since we left the road. Just as I was becoming convinced we'd wandered off course, the dark shape of what I was sure was Humpback Hill appeared up ahead.

A flashlight snapped on and created a white carpet of light.

"We're far enough away now, for sure," Grandpa said. "Who should lead?"

"Buzz," I suggested. "He knows the way better than any of us."

Buzz took the lead and turned on his flashlight as well. Beth fell in behind, then me and Grandpa took up the rear. With Buzz in the lead and the light to guide us we began moving much faster. The only sounds were our feet scuffing against the ground and Grandpa's loud breathing from behind me. I turned around. His face looked strained and he was puffing.

"Could we take a break?" I asked.

Buzz stopped. We pulled out our water bottles and Grandpa and I sat down on some rocks. He looked tired and despite the chill in the air he was sweating. I didn't need a break but planned on sitting here until he'd caught his breath.

I wanted to take a deep, long sip of water, but I thought about how hot it was yesterday and how we might need all the water we'd brought along. I took a shallow sip and re-sealed the container.

"Let's get back in motion," Grandpa suggested.

Buzz and Beth got back on their feet and I remained seated.

"You looking for a special invitation?" Beth asked.

"No . . . maybe we should move a little slower though."

"Why, is the baby tired?" she asked.

"No!" I snapped and then stopped myself before I said anything more. "It's just that I think we need to be careful. What if somebody trips and sprains an ankle or something?"

"He has a point," Buzz said.

Even in the dim light I could tell that Beth didn't look pleased with him agreeing with me.

"Sure, whatever," she said.

Buzz took the lead and we followed. We moved until the cliff practically flattened itself to the ground before we climbed aboard the whale. We settled into the very centre, well away from the edges, and then Grandpa told us to turn off the flashlights. It instantly got impossibly dark and we stopped moving because we couldn't see anything more than a few feet in front of us. Gradually, my eyes had a chance to readjust to the darkness. The sky was completely clear now and the light of ten million little twinkling stars and a big, full moon seemed to light up the entire slope. Even though I could now see enough to move, I had the urge to just stand completely still and gaze up into the night sky.

I started to think that maybe getting here was better than arriving. Soon we might find treasure, but we might find nothing. At least on the way we still had hope. If I was wrong we'd have nothing.

"You coming or what?" Beth called out.

The three of them had started to move and were now a few dozen feet farther along. I trotted after them.

As we went, I gradually found myself straying over to one side. Up front and over the side I could see where the town sat in the dark distance. There were a few pinpricks of light, not much bigger or brighter than the stars. They marked the little flickers of street or porch lights that were burning through the night.

As I continued to watch, I noticed that some of the lights seemed to be getting closer, seemed to be moving. At first, I figured it was just my eyes playing tricks on me, but soon there was no mistaking it. Six white lights, three pairs, were coming out this way. Almost instantly I realized what they were: cars rolling along the road from town to the Money Pit.

"There are some cars coming along the road!" I called out.

Beth and Buzz scrambled over to have a look. Grandpa came more slowly.

"I can't see anything," Buzz complained.

"I see 'em," Grandpa said. "Out there, coming along the road from town."

"More police?" I asked.

"Not all three of them. The whole island only has

four police cars. One's already passed and a second one isn't going anywhere for a while, so maybe two of those are police. I wonder if your mother is in one of the cars?"

"Why would Mom be there?" Beth asked.

"My guess is they went and woke her up right after I rammed that cruiser. I'm sure Gus noticed you kids in the truck as well so I'm sure she knows you're with me."

I swallowed hard. Worrying her, and getting her mad, hadn't been part of the plan at all. It was never part of any of my plans. It seemed I spent most of my life keeping everybody calm.

"Do you think your parents know already, too?" Beth asked Buzz.

"Maybe. Mom says she has so many kids she wouldn't notice if a few wandered off. I hope she wasn't just joking."

"Best way to stop them from worrying is to go home . . . with the treasure. Let's get going again," Grandpa suggested.

It didn't take long for the slope to level off. We'd reached the top. We stopped at the edge of the "blowhole."

"This is it," I announced.

Grandpa started chuckling to himself. "You know, when I was a boy, my friends and I always used to come here. We'd build fires and a couple of times we even set up tents and spent the night right here," he said, pointing down into the depression. "We'd tell each other stories about lots of things, including

Captain Kidd and the Money Pit. Is that where you found the skull?"

"Yeah, right in the centre," I answered.

Buzz leaped down onto the sand and Beth passed down the tools she was carrying. I tossed down my shovel and bucket. Carefully, Grandpa put his feet over the edge and lowered himself the four or five feet to the bottom.

"Do you want me to light the lantern now?" Buzz asked.

"Probably better not to. Being high up like this means we can see in all directions, but I'm afraid it also means we can be *seen* from all directions. The light just might shine up into the sky like a beacon, or at least like those headlights coming along the road."

"There's enough light, anyway," I added, looking up at the full moon.

I dug the shovel into the sand, heaved it up and tossed the load over the side of the rocks. We'd begun. Part of me couldn't help thinking about Mom and what was happening for her and how I should be home tucked into my bed. But the other part figured there was no place in the whole world I'd rather be at that moment. I was out here treasure hunting and all that lay between us and the treasure was some sand . . . and at least one headless skeleton.

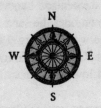

Chapter Twenty-Nine

The coolness of the night air was soon burned away by the heat I was generating with the shovel. Beth and Buzz and I were all digging while Grandpa worked to string the tarp up so it formed a roof over our heads. It got darker and harder to work as he continued to put it in place, but when he was satisfied it would block out most of the light that would be thrown skyward he said it would be okay to light the lantern. Its light filled the hole, making it as bright as day.

In the two hours we'd been digging we'd taken the hole down another three feet and I could now jump straight up and still not see over the top of the rocks. Getting deeper was the idea, but now each shovelful of sand had to be tossed a lot higher and of course get through the small gap left by the tarp. More than a couple of times one of us had tossed a shovel of sand skyward and it hadn't made the edge and tumbled back onto everybody's heads. And I was becoming even more concerned about Grandpa. He was keeping pace with Buzz, hefting shovels full of sand over the top. But he was too old to be straining like that. I wanted this to be a treasure dig . . . not his grave. A shudder went up my spine.

I had to think about something else, too, as I dug in the shovel. I was digging as far off to the side as I could. I didn't want to be the one to find the rest of the skeleton. At least this way I'd have a little time to react to it . . . thud, my shovel clanked into something solid. My mind raced to the obvious conclusion. I had the urge to just pull my shovel free, walk across to the other side and start digging there, pretending I hadn't hit anything. I couldn't do that.

"Grandpa I've hit something."

"What sort of something?" he asked as he came over and dropped to one knee by my shovel. Buzz continued to dig, while Beth had stopped working and was watching.

"I don't know . . . but it's hard."

"Could be a rock," he suggested.

"Or the treasure," Beth chipped in.

Or a human bone, I thought, but didn't say.

Grandpa started to scoop away the sand with his hands until he'd formed a small opening all around my shovel.

"Pull your shovel out and let me have a look," he ordered.

He leaned down farther. "I got something all right. Feels sort of smooth . . . and round."

All I could think was that he'd unearthed a second skull.

Grandpa grunted as he tried to pull the object free. Maybe I should be trying to get it myself so he wouldn't have to strain . . . what was I talking about, grabbing a skull or a human bone with my bare hands?

"It's moving . . . it's moving . . . here it comes!"

I stepped back as he held it up. It was a rock.

"Oh, that's a relief!" I exclaimed.

"A relief? It's a disappointment," Beth said. "I was thinking it was treasure. What did you think it was?"

"I guess I . . . sort of thought . . . you know, that maybe it was a skull or another part of a skeleton," I admitted sheepishly.

"You mean, like this," Buzz asked.

We all turned to him. In one hand he was holding his shovel while in the other he held a bone that was as long as his forearm. I backed away a half step.

"There's a couple more here as well that are still partially buried," Buzz added.

Grandpa rushed over to look. Beth craned her neck but looked like she didn't want to get much closer than she already was. I was pretty happy to be some distance from any and all human bones that weren't inside my body.

"Sam, pass me over one of the buckets," Grandpa ordered.

I turned back and grabbed one. I took a couple of

steps and reached out, way out, to hand it to him. He took the bone from Buzz and dropped it into the bucket with a clang.

"From now on this is going to be like eating a bucket of chicken. This here is the bone bucket. Any bone you find goes right in here," Grandpa explained with a chuckle.

"We're just going to pile them in there?" Beth questioned.

"Only thing I can think of. Normally you're supposed to call in the coroner when you find human remains, but we can't be doing that, so we'll do the best we can."

There was a loud clunk as Buzz deposited a second bone into the bottom of the bucket. "And there's more where those came from," he added. He sounded cheerful.

I was sure he was right. I'd heard that the human body had more than a hundred bones, and so far we'd only found three.

Grandpa turned off the lantern. The sun, invisible from where we worked in the hole, had obviously peeked over the horizon and seeped in around the tarp, flooding the area with daylight. I looked up and my eyes were stung by blowing sand. It was piled high on top of the rocks and the wind was whipping it back into the hole.

"I'm going to go up top and move the sand away from the edge," I said to everybody as I started to scale the side of the pit.

As I climbed, I cast one eye back to the bone bucket. It sat off to the far side and was overflowing with bones. Grandpa figured we'd pretty well found the entire remains of one man, with a little extra to spare. I didn't like the sound of that because it meant a second skull was still buried in there. I'd almost gotten used to the other bones, but something about skulls—unmistakably human—was different.

I reached the top and stretched. The sun was just above the horizon, a flaming ball in a cloudless sky. It was going to be awfully hot down there before we were done. I struck my shovel into the mound of sand ringing the hole. At least here I didn't have to heave it up eight or ten feet, but just over to the side.

As I stood there, staring into the distance as much as moving sand, Grandpa climbed out over the rim.

"I thought you could use a hand up here. It's getting a bit crowded for three people down there anyway," he said.

He started pushing away sand with the side of his foot. Then, for no reason that I could see, he began to chuckle to himself and that chuckle became a laugh.

"Are you . . . are you all right?" I asked hesitantly.

"All right? Not all right, at all. Much better than all right. And I have you to thank for that," he answered.

"Me?"

He nodded his head. "Not too many hours ago was the lowest point in my life. The Money Pit had come up empty, all the bills I hadn't paid were getting ready to crash down on my head, my licence was taken away, and I felt like an old fool." He paused and put a hand on my shoulder. "But now here I am with my grandkids, out in the middle of nowhere, digging for pirate treasure. And you know, I can't think of any place I'd rather be or anything I'd rather be doing right now."

"Me neither," I said.

"So I may be a fool, but at least I feel like a *young* fool."

"You're not a fool!" I protested.

"It's hard to argue. Look at all the darn foolish things I've done."

"We couldn't have done this without you. Do you think a fool could have gotten away from the police, or figured out how to lay a false trail, or organized the dig?"

He nodded his head in agreement. "Some things I can still do well, but you'd think different if you'd seen my old pappy at the end."

"How old are you, Grandpa?" I asked.

"Is this another one of those questions to see if I'm too daft to know my own age?"

"No, I just want to know."

"I'll be seventy-eight on my next birthday."

"And how old was your father when he died?"

"He nearly lived to the century mark. He died a few days before his hundredth birthday. It was a shame, he always said he wanted to see his second century."

"And you said he was only funny in the head for the last few years of his life, right?"

"Well he slowed down in his eighties, but it was

only the last two or . . ." He stopped talking and a smile creased his face. "And I'm still almost twenty years away from reaching his age."

"Exactly!" I beamed.

"But how do you explain some of the things I've done? I'm certain to lose my house now because I didn't pay the bills."

"But you didn't pay the bills because you were certain the treasure was in the pit. You would have been a fool *not* to invest your money!"

Grandpa took his other arm and wrapped it around me, holding me in a tight hug. I could feel the bones of his chest sticking through his clothes.

"I want to thank you, Sam, for making everything right."

"But we haven't found the treasure yet."

"It doesn't matter if all we find is a bucket of bones," he answered. There was a catch in his voice and I knew he was close to tears. I was close to tears as well.

"But what about your house?"

"It's just a house. I can live someplace else. Your mother said something about me coming to live with you."

"You leaving the island? I just can't imagine you not being here."

"Neither can I, but I guess I'd rather be someplace else with the three of you instead of here without you."

"But what about the police . . . about jail?"

"They're not going to put me in jail. I'm an old

man. And besides, they say I'm too old and batty to know what I'm doing so how can they put me in jail? I'll just tell 'em I'm crazy as a jay bird. Anyway, who says there isn't treasure down there in this hole? You keep working up here and I'll go down and see how things are going."

Grandpa loosened his hug and carefully lowered himself into the hole, leaving me alone to finish shifting the sand away from the lip of the excavation. I walked over to the very rim of the hill. Off in one direction I saw the Money Pit. The yellow fence still marked the boundaries, but there was no movement inside the compound. Even the asphalt factory was still and the sky above was blue and unblemished by smoke.

In the other direction sat the town. I pictured people moving around in their houses and the stores opening and the police making a plan to figure out where we were. And of course Mom was there somewhere. I wondered what she was doing right now, and how she was feeling, and what she was thinking, and what would happen to us when we got home.

Then on the horizon, or I guess just above the horizon, I saw movement. It was small and shimmering in the sun. It was moving fast and had to be some kind of plane. The island didn't have an airport, but a few times I'd seen sea planes land in the harbour and taxi right up to the dock to let off people and packages.

I watched as it came across the sky. It seemed to be following the road out from town to the Money Pit. As it came closer, its image became clearer and I could tell it wasn't a plane, but a helicopter. It was closing in fast and I could even see there were markings on the side. Maybe it belonged to the people at the pit, or was bringing people for a tour of the island or . . . all at once the markings on the side of the copter were clear: POLICE. It was a police helicopter and it was probably looking for us!

Suddenly, the helicopter veered off sharply to the side and headed straight toward where I stood exposed and alone and so visible. I ran back to the hole, scrambled into the opening and rolled down the rocky sides, plopping down in the soft sand at the bottom.

"You have to be more careful," Grandpa stated in a concerned voice as he helped me to my feet.

"There's a helicopter!" I screamed. "A police helicopter and it's coming this way!"

"Did it see you?" he asked.

"I'm not sure, but maybe," I answered. Actually, I was pretty sure it had seen me, and that was the reason it changed direction, but I couldn't bring myself to say it.

Grandpa opened his mouth, but before he could speak the sound of the chopper splashed down the opening and filled the hole. Beth dropped her shovel and came and stood close to Grandpa. Up above the hole it appeared for a brief moment, hovering, its shadow cast into the hole and on top of us, and then it moved slowly off to the side and out of view. Maybe they hadn't seen me. But how could they miss the tarp strung out across the top of the hole?

"ATTENTION! THIS IS THE POLICE!" screamed a metallic voice. "COME OUT AND IDENTIFY YOURSELF!"

I pushed my mouth against Grandpa's ear and cupped my hands to shield my voice against the crushing sound of the helicopter.

"What do we do?" I screamed.

"We're going to go up top . . . you and me," he yelled back. "And we're going to make them go away. Grab a shovel!"

Chapter Thirty

Make them go away? He and I were going to chase away a police helicopter with a couple of shovels? What was he talking about?

Grandpa half-pushed, half-dragged me up the incline. I was shocked at the strength of his grip on my arm and the power with which he was propelling me along. But even more, I was impressed with his sheer determination. He made me almost believe we could make the helicopter go away. I shot out of the opening, dragging the shovel, and fought my way through the wind and noise of the helicopter. It was even louder up here, and I was being assaulted by the sound and the thousands of grains of sand, whipped up by the spinning rotors, pelting painfully against my face.

"MR. SIMMONS, THIS IS SHERIFF O'BRIEN. WE'RE GOING TO PUT DOWN," called out the loudspeaker of the helicopter.

"Over my dead body!" Grandpa screamed back. His voice would have been lost to them but his gestures were unmistakable as he shook his fists in the air.

He ran to a spot right under the descending craft and started to wave his shovel in the air. The helicopter continued to come lower and looked like it was going to land right on top of Grandpa! He reached up with his shovel and there was a loud whack as he struck it against one of the landing gears. Instantly, the copter's engines grew louder and it veered upward and away. Was he totally insane? You can't attack a police helicopter! Then again, maybe you can't smash up a police car, either.

Grandpa motioned for me to come to his side. In stunned disbelief, I stumbled across the rock face to him. He cupped his hands over my ear. "This is the only spot on the top of the rock where it's flat enough and wide enough for them to set down. We can't let them! Wave your shovel in the air!"

He started running in little circles, his shovel in the air. Above him hovered the helicopter. I couldn't help thinking of a knight holding his sword aloft to fight off a flying dragon. I ran out to him and waved my sword skyward, too.

"MR. SIMMONS YOU ARE ENDANGERING THE LIVES OF YOURSELF AND YOUR

GRANDSON! STOP IMMEDIATELY OR YOU WILL BE FACING ADDITIONAL CRIMINAL CHARGES OF RESISTING ARREST AND CHILD ENDANGERMENT!"

I stopped for an instant. Grandpa continued with even more enthusiasm, keeping the copter at bay. I lowered my shovel. We couldn't do this. It was—

"Don't stop, Sam!" he yelled.

I hesitated for a split second and then lifted my shovel up in the air again.

"Good, we're not going to let those—"

He stopped as the helicopter lifted higher and veered off to the side. Grandpa dropped the shovel and picked up a rock. He heaved it toward the chopper and to my amazement it pinged off the undercarriage of the craft. As the helicopter swooped off to the side and the sound faded away, he whooped and did a victory dance.

"We have to get back to the hole, quickly!" Grandpa exclaimed, picking up his fallen shovel. "They're just looking for another place to set it down and they'll be up here as soon as they can. We don't have much time!"

"But shouldn't we try to get away?" I suggested.

"Get away? We have no chance of getting away. What we have to do is get to the treasure before they get here."

"The treasure's not important now. We can get it later," I said.

"No, we can't! You don't understand! The secret's

going to be out now. We can only claim this as our treasure if we find it! If they get here before we unearth something then anybody can continue digging here and whoever finds even a single coin can claim the whole site!"

"But that's not fair!" I protested. Of all the things in life that seemed unfair, this seemed like the biggest . . . and I was tired of things being unfair.

"Fair or not, that's just the way it is. We have to dig, and dig like our lives depend upon it . . . dig like Captain Kidd himself is chasing behind us with his cutlass in hand!"

I raced ahead of Grandpa and plunged down the hole, sliding and scraping myself on the rock side. I landed with a thud and bumped Beth off her feet.

"Dig! Dig! We have to dig!" I screamed and dug my shovel into the sand, hurling a shovelful skyward.

"What are you talking about?" Beth asked, picking herself up off the ground.

"The police are going to be here in a while. . . I don't know how long . . . it depends on where they have to land!" I heaved another shovelful over the edge. "And we have to find the treasure before they come and take us away!"

"But . . ." Buzz started to say.

"But nothing! If we don't find something before they get here then anybody can continue digging and claim the treasure for themselves!"

Before Buzz could utter another word, we were thrown into blinding light. I shielded my eyes and looked up. Grandpa stood at the top of the hill, knife in hand, with the tarp partially cut free and hanging partway down the stony slope.

"They put down about a fifteen-minute walk from here. Put your backs into it!" he bellowed.

Buzz and I dug in our shovels and Beth bent down and used the pail as a scoop. She tossed the attached rope up to Grandpa and he started to pull it up to the top. I hurled another shovelful skyward; some sand escaped over the top while more than half rolled back down the sides again. Buzz threw a load up and it cleared the top and disappeared. I dug my shovel in again and it punched through a thin layer of sand and crunched into the solid rock of the slanting side.

"Keep digging," Grandpa yelled down to us. "I'm going to go down and delay them as long as I can."

"What are you going to do?" I called out.

"I don't know yet. Maybe talk to them, or give myself up, or run off and make them chase me, or hit them with a stick, or fake a heart attack. I don't know, but I do know I'm not going to let them get up here without a fight!"

"Good luck!" I yelled out as his head disappeared from view.

Beth slumped down to the ground. "I can't get the sand over the top. It's too high."

"I can't either. You go up top and pull the buckets up and I'll stay down here and load them. Buzz, can you keep digging?"

He snorted and his answer was to throw another shovel load of sand over the top. Quickly, I filled one bucket and then the second while Beth strained to get the first one to the top. I dropped to my knees and used my hands to scoop another handful of sand from the pit and tossed it straight up in the air. It reached the top and was blown away.

"How many feet do you think we have to go?" Buzz panted.

"I don't know, but we have to keep going. No matter what happens we can't stop digging. If they get by Grandpa, Beth and I will go and meet them before they get to the hole. Maybe they don't know you're missing, or that you're with us. You have to keep going!"

"I'm not stopping, no matter what. Captain Kidd himself couldn't get me out of this hole. The treasure is ours and nobody is taking it away from us!"

Maybe Beth wasn't thrilled with Buzz anymore, but I was starting to like him again like in the old times.

He dug his shovel into the sand again and another few inches were removed. He and I kept digging, pushing in our shovels and tossing the sand up the stony side. I was starting to feel the increased pace—my arms were aching and sweat was pouring down my sides. I didn't know how long I could keep this up.

"Sam, they're coming!" Beth called out. "They're coming up the back!"

I looked over at Buzz. "Keep going."

He nodded and dug in again. On all fours I climbed up the side of the hole. It was now over ten feet deep. Beth stood off to the side, staring at the approaching men. There were four men in uniforms. Grandpa was nowhere to be seen.

"Come on," I said as I walked by her and toward them.

"What are you doing?" she asked as she scrambled to my side.

"We've got to give Buzz some more time."

"What's the point? It's over," Beth said forlornly.

"Don't say that! It's not over yet!"

I grabbed her by the hand and pulled her down the back of the whale toward the approaching men. It was a strange sensation, rushing toward them when I had absolutely no idea what I was going to say or do when we got there. I looked down the slope. They were coming up quickly despite the incline. They were now so close that I could see the angry expressions on their faces.

"Where's our Grandpa?" I demanded furiously, the words popping out before I thought about them.

My tone seemed to throw them for a second. They stopped moving and we continued down toward them, farther away from the hole and Buzz.

"We're worried about our Grandpa," I repeated. "Where is he?"

"We have him down below. He's being taken to the chopper," one of the officers finally answered.

"We need to see him to make sure he's okay. Please take us to him right away," I pleaded.

"Sure thing," he said. He turned to two of his men. "Take them down to their grandfather."

They started toward us and one tried to take me by the arm. I shook free and bounded a few steps away.

"What are the rest of you going to do?" I questioned.

"We're going up to the top to get your other friend."

"He's already gone. He left this morning before you got here," Beth lied.

"Is that right? Well, I guess we'll just have to go up and see for ourselves," he said. Obviously, he hadn't believed Beth.

"You can't!" I barked.

"We can't? And why is that?" he asked.

I took a few steps until I stood smack dab between them and the path to the hole.

"Because . . . because I'm not going to let you," I said angrily.

Beth looked at me in wide-mouthed shock.

Two of the men started to snort and snicker and a third burst out in laughter. At least I'd slowed them down for a few seconds to laugh at me.

"Kid's as crazy as his grandfather," one of the officers said to the other.

"Shut up!" I yelled. "Nobody as stupid as you has any right to say anything about my Grandpa!"

The officer looked shocked and then angry while the others laughed at his expense.

"Come on kid, don't make this any harder. Grab them!" he ordered.

One officer shot out a hand and grabbed Beth while a second lunged for me. I skittered backward, almost tripping over a rock, but regained my balance in time to scramble away from his outstretched arms. A second officer leaped forward, but I dodged him as well as he tripped over his thick-soled boots.

I ran back toward the hole as three of them came after me. I screeched to a stop at the lip of the hole. Turning back around, I saw them closing in on me rapidly. They looked incredibly angry. Even more angry than those security guards. I bent down and picked up one of the buckets. With all my might I hurled it through the air. It bounced a couple of times and whacked into the shins of one of the men. He howled in pain. Without stopping to think I picked up the other bucket. It was full. I threw the load of sand at them. The wind whipped it at them and the officers recoiled as the grains found their eyes and mouths. I then tossed the now-empty bucket and was shocked by the force of my throw as it sailed right over the head of one of the startled men. They'd be on top of me in just seconds.

"Have you found anything, Buzz?" I screamed desperately.

"Nothing, nothing at all!" he yelled back as another shovelful of sand burst over the side.

"It's all over, kid!" snarled one of the officers.

He was right. There was no place to go. They had me trapped and surrounded.

I looked down and Buzz looked up. He shrugged. It was over.

Then, in the bottom of the hole, just over from

Buzz, I saw something shining up at me, reflecting the brilliant sunlight.

"That's all, kid," the officer said as he reached out once again to take me by the arm.

I turned away and dove head first into the hole. I heard the officer gasp in surprise. Buzz's eyes got wide in shock and then he reached out to try to cushion my fall. I fell well short of him and my legs thumped against the rock side with a terrible shock. I started to roll, feeling the sharp edges and points digging into me, before I landed in the soft sand at the bottom.

"Are you crazy, kid?" the officer yelled down the hole.

Buzz reached out and offered me a hand. I brushed by him and on all fours scurried across the ground. I dug one hand into the sand and pulled something free . . . a handful of somethings . . . gold coins.

Chapter Thirty-One

"Come on, sleepy-head, it's time to get up."

My mother's voice was soft and gentle and the last thing I wanted to do was get out of bed. I just wanted to roll over and dream some more about the treasure and . . . I sat bolt upright in bed, my eyes wide open. I knew it wasn't a dream.

Mom and Grandpa were standing in my bedroom door. Both of them had silly grins plastered on their faces.

"How long have I been asleep?" I asked.

"Almost eighteen hours," Mom answered.

"Eighteen hours!"

"I guess you were making up for the sleep you lost the other night," Mom said.

"The treasure . . . what's happening to the trea-sure?"

"It's fine. At least the part they've brought up. They're still bringing more up right now," Grandpa said.

"What do you mean they? It's our treasure isn't it?" I demanded.

"Don't worry, don't worry," Grandpa said. "It's ours. Yours and Beth's and Buzz's and mine." His face broke into a huge smile. "I have some men who are working for us. One of the things about being rich is you can get people to do the hard things for you."

"We're rich?" I asked hesitantly.

"Definitely rich. Only question is how rich, but we won't know that until the treasure is all dug out," Grandpa answered.

"That's wonder . . ." I stopped. "But what about the police? Are they putting you in jail?"

"Nope, no jail. I promised them a brand-new police car, apologized, turned over the keys to my truck, and told 'em I wouldn't drive again unless I passed a new test."

"And that made it okay?" I questioned.

"Amazing how finding a treasure makes everything all right," Grandpa chuckled.

"How will you get around without a truck?" I asked.

"Oh, I wouldn't go worrying about that," he said as he slipped an arm around Mom's waist and gave her a squeeze.

"I'll be here to pick up groceries and drive your grandfather places," Mom said.

I gasped and looked at her and then at Grandpa

and back at her once more. "You mean for the next few weeks, right?"

"I mean for the next few years," Mom said.

"We're going to be staying on the island?"

"We pretty well have to. I can't take the ferry everyday to work at my new job here on the island," Mom explained.

"Your new job!"

"Yes, I'll be teaching grade six here at the island school."

"When did that happen?" I asked in shock.

"I applied for it last week. Remember when I had to rush out for an appointment? That was the job interview."

"But why didn't you tell us?" I asked.

"There was nothing to tell. Besides, I didn't want to get anybody's hopes up until I knew. I didn't get word I got the job until yesterday."

"You mean we were always going to stay here?" I asked. "Stay with Grandpa?"

She nodded.

I leaped out of bed and wrapped my arms around both of them.

"I'm thrilled you're staying, but I've been telling her she really doesn't have to work," Grandpa said. "We're rich!"

"Not we," Mom corrected me. "Maybe Sam and Beth and you, and even Buzz, but not me. I have to work for a living."

"But, Mom!"

"But, Mom, nothing. It's not like you're going to see much of that money, anyway," she said.

"But I thought it was all ours?"

"It is, but most of your and Beth's share of the money is going into a trust fund that neither of you can touch until you're twenty-one years old. And don't even think about arguing with me! Besides, I love teaching and I don't know what I'd do with myself if I didn't have something to do everyday."

"She's right," Grandpa agreed. "A person has to keep their mind active if they want to keep it working. Use it or lose it."

"What are you going to do now that the treasure's been found?" I asked.

"There'll be months and months of work until we're finished bringing it all up," he said.

"And then?"

"Well . . . all I can say for sure is *one* treasure's been found. I heard there are others all over the island. You wouldn't happen to be interested in a little treasure hunt, would you?" he asked.